She caught at his arm but he shook her hand away. Becky's eyes filled with tears. This was worse, far worse than she had ever imagined. There was nothing she could say that would make Nick feel better. The plain fact was, she had a job, a future, and at the moment, he didn't. No wonder he sounded bitter. She'd have felt the same, in his place. But...

But he's supposed to love me, care about me, said a clear little voice in her head. Couldn't he even *pretend* to be pleased for me?

She tried again. "London's only an hour and a half away on the train," she pointed out. "I shall be coming home for weekends, Nick. It's not as though we won't be able to see each other. I mean, you could come down to London as well..."

Her voice trailed away. She could hardly bear to watch him, hunched into his old cord jacket, his untidy brown hair spilling down over the collar. How many times had she brushed that hair back from his face, run her fingers lovingly through it? But now...

Her breath caught on a sob.

Point Romance

Breaking Away

Jill Eckersley

■ SCHOLASTIC

Scholastic Children's Books
Commonwealth House, 1–19 New Oxford Street,
London WC1A 1NU, UK
a division of Scholastic Ltd
London ~ New York ~ Toronto ~ Sydney ~ Auckland

First published in the UK by Scholastic Ltd, 1997
Copyright © Jill Eckersley, 1997

ISBN 0 590 19121 7

Typeset by TW Typesetting, Midsomer Norton, Somerset
Printed by Cox & Wyman Ltd, Reading, Berks.

10 9 8 7 6 5 4 3 2 1

1

"Hi, Becky!"

"Jan! Come in, you look fantastic, you're so brown!" Becky Rivers flung the front door wide to let her friend in. As she led the way up the stairs to her bedroom, she went on, "How does it feel to be back? Crete sounded brilliant, from your postcard. I bet you didn't want to come home, did you?"

Jan laughed as Becky opened her bedroom door and the two girls flopped down on Becky's divan. "Heather didn't," Jan admitted. "She met this incredible guy. Panos, his name was. Talk about a Greek god, he was gorgeous."

"What about you?" Becky demanded. "Don't tell me you didn't have a holiday romance, in two whole weeks? You didn't leave all the hunky guys to your sister, did you?"

Jan wrinkled her freckled nose. "Well, there was Theo ... he was pretty cool, but he didn't speak very much English and I got a bit bored with the shall-we-dance-would-you-like-drink-I-walk-you-home-we-meet-tomorrow sort of conversations," said Jan. "I met two lovely guys called Dave and Matt from Liverpool, though. They're in a band. They were a real laugh ... hang on, I've brought some photos to show you..."

She scrabbled around in her shoulder-bag for the wallet of photographs.

Becky lay back against the pillows, smiling. It was good to have Jan back. She'd really missed her, these last two weeks. Two days previously she had seen Louise, her other best friend, off to Australia with her parents. She, Jan and Louise had met on their first day at the comprehensive and had gone up the school together, side by side. In July, after A levels, they'd left, and Becky knew that nothing would ever be quite the same again. Louise was on the other side of the world, where her father had a new job, Jan was beginning a secretarial course, while she, Becky... She heaved a deep sigh.

"Whatever's the matter?" Jan said, her smile fading. "Becky? What is it? Something's wrong, isn't it? You idiot, you should've said something straight away, not let me go rambling on about Theo and Heather and Panos and... What *is* it?"

Becky reached into the drawer of her bedside cabinet and pulled out a long white envelope. "Read this," she said, handing it to Jan.

Jan looked puzzled, but pulled out the letter and began to read. After a few seconds she gasped and flung the letter down on Becky's bed. "I don't believe it!" she shrieked. "You've got the job! You lucky, lucky thing, that's amazing! Aren't you thrilled? I'd be over the moon if it was me... Becky?"

Oh, no, Becky thought. Jan's going to think I'm crazy too, just like Louise did, and Mum and Dad. I hoped she'd understand...

"Becky?" Jan repeated. She spoke very slowly, as if Becky was a five-year-old, or someone who didn't understand English. "Becky, this is a letter from the Features Editor of a national magazine, offering you a job as Junior Assistant in the Features Department, on three months' trial. A job, Becky! Not work experience, like you had in the summer, but a proper full-time job. And not just any old job but the job you've always wanted to do. It's a chance in a million. It is, isn't it?"

"Yes," Becky admitted simply.

"So ... why are you looking so miserable about it? What's wrong? When I went away, you were on pins waiting for this what's-her-name, Linda Hobson, to write and let you know whether you'd got the job or not."

"I know," said Becky.

"So what's the problem?"

"Nick," said Becky.

For a moment, Jan looked exasperated. Then she put a sympathetic hand on Becky's arm.

"Oh Becky," she said, more gently. "What did he say when you told him?"

Becky shook her head. "That's just it," she said. "I haven't told him yet. For one thing, the letter only arrived on Monday, and for another, well, I just don't know what to say."

3

Jan was silent for a moment. "Well," she said practically, "the sooner you tell him the better, I would say. You can't put it off for ever, can you? He'll have to know sometime, and far better that he hears it from you than from one of the others. That *would* be awful."

"I ... I know," said Becky unhappily. "I haven't actually told many people. Only Mum and Dad, and Louise before she went away, and now you. I know Nick should be one of the first to know. He is my boyfriend, after all. But..."

"I know," said Jan. "How d'you think he'll take it?"

Becky shrugged. "Who knows?" she said. "Honestly, Jan, it's almost as though I don't know him any more. Ever since the A level results came it's like he was a different person."

She paused for a moment, her thoughts winging back to the day the results had come, changing her life for ever. Until then, everything had been fine between Nick and herself. Nick knew she wanted to be a journalist. He'd always known that, as well as applying for college courses in media studies, she'd written to lots of magazine editors asking if there were any junior opportunities going. Most had replied with a discouraging "thanks but no thanks". Only Linda Hobson had offered her two weeks' unpaid work experience in her summer holidays.

The two weeks had happened to coincide with Nick's trip to North Wales, rock-climbing with his friend Pete Ransome, so they'd arranged to phone each other on alternate evenings. He'd seemed pleased for her, interested in what she had to say about the job and the friendly girls she worked with, almost as excited as she was when Linda, the Features Editor, hinted that there might be a permanent job going.

Nick was studying science A levels and had applied for engineering courses at several London colleges, so that he and Becky could be near each other. They had their future all planned, all worked out... Then, the day after they returned home, the results came out...

And Nick had failed. Not just by a few points, so that some of the colleges he'd applied for might still have considered him, but totally, utterly, and spectacularly. He had been so shattered that Becky hadn't liked to ask him what had gone wrong.

She could still hardly bear to think about that fateful day. She'd rushed up to school, her heart in her mouth, to join the others clustered round the notice-boards in the Hall. She, Jan and Louise had flung their arms round one another and burst into tears of joy and relief when they saw their results. They had only just mopped up and started looking around for everyone else when Becky saw Nick, late as usual, push his way though the crowd and run his finger down the list of names. He'd looked ... looked again ... then turned and walked away.

"Nick?" Becky had said. "I passed, with a starred A in English, look, and Jan passed too, and Louise..."

He turned round, and she knew she would always remember the look on his face.

"Nick?" she repeated.

He didn't meet her eyes.

Becky ran after him and caught his arm. "Nick, what is it?" she faltered.

"I failed," he said simply.

Becky gasped. "Failed? All of them? Oh Nick..."

"Yup," said Nick. There was an awful, embarrassed silence.

"I ... I'm so sorry. I don't know what to say," said Becky awkwardly.

Nick shrugged. "Yeah. Well, that's how it goes," he said.

Becky longed to put her arms round him, tell him it didn't matter, tell him he could do re-sits, that he'd get another chance, and that she loved him anyway, but she didn't dare. Even if they hadn't been in the school hall, surrounded by other students and staff, she could sense that pity was the last thing Nick wanted.

Anyway, how could she say it didn't matter? Everyone knew it did, that exam passes were vital if you wanted any kind of career. And even if he re-sat the exams, he wouldn't be able to get into college till next year, and where did that leave their plans to stay together? Even if she didn't get a job straight away, her grades were good enough to get her into any of the colleges she'd applied to. She'd be going off to London, and he'd be stuck at home. Some relationships survived that sort of separation, she knew they did, with couples a hundred miles or more apart.

But a lot didn't.

It hadn't got any better in the weeks since the

results came. For the first time since she and Nick had known each other, Becky found him difficult to talk to. She didn't like to mention everyone else's plans for work or college, and since that was pretty much all anyone talked about, what was there to say? Pete Ransome, Nick's best friend since junior school, was going to art college in Liverpool. Felicity Jones, who'd got a string of A grades, was trying for an Oxford scholarship. Tim Collingwood was going to work in a bank. Suzanne Chalmers was going in for nursing, Jan was taking a secretarial course and Louise was off to Australia.

Everyone seemed to know exactly what they were doing, except Becky ... and Nick. When Linda Hobson's letter came, it seemed like the last straw. When she saw the magazine's logo on the envelope her heart had leapt into her mouth. She'd opened it with shaking fingers.

"Becky? Is it the job?" her mum had asked.

"Yes. Oh Mum... I've got it! They want me to start in two weeks. I can't believe it!" Becky gasped.

There were kisses and congratulations all round and even Emily, Becky's three-year-old sister, banged her spoon on the table as she became caught up in the general excitement. I've actually been offered a job on a magazine, Becky thought to herself. I never dreamed I'd be so lucky. They must have liked me, even though I didn't seem to do much in my work experience weeks except make tea and do the filing!

The only problem was – Nick.

She'd told him that she'd applied for the job, of course, but how could she tell him she'd actually got it? "Well, the best of luck," he had said, smiling at her – but his smile didn't quite reach his eyes. Suddenly, Becky felt very, very fond of him.

Dear Nick, shambling, untidy, with hair that always looked slightly in need of cutting, and the big brown puppy-dog eyes that had been almost the first thing she'd noticed about him. They'd been together for nearly a year, had known one another for almost three. Becky loved him, or at least, she supposed she did.

To begin with, she had tried to push thoughts of the future – their future – out of her mind. Some couples who had been together all through school, stayed together afterwards as well. And it was hard to imagine a future without Nick. They were such good friends, as well as being boy- and girl-friend. Or they had been, until Nick's results came and he'd turned into a moody, silent stranger before her eyes. She sighed again. Everything was changing. She and Nick would have to change, too. Or would they? Could they?

"Well, I think it's a shame," Jan said.

Becky blinked. "Sorry, Jan, I was miles away," she apologized. "What's a shame?"

"You," said Jan. "Here you are, being offered this fantastic opportunity. I mean, jobs like that don't come up very often, do they? And instead of being excited about it, you're drooping around like a wet weekend."

Becky frowned. "I know," she said. "If it wasn't

for telling Nick ... or if he hadn't failed his exams, if he was coming to London as well, everything would be brilliant..."

"That's an awful lot of ifs," Jan put in gently. "And besides, I think you're looking on the black side, you know, Becky. If Nick really loves you, he won't stand in your way. He knows you want to be a journalist, doesn't he? He knows there was a job going and that you'd applied for it?"

"Yes, he knows," Becky agreed.

"Well, then. It's only London you're going to, after all, not the far side of the moon. It's only a hundred miles away. You can come home every weekend to see Nick if you want to. Or he can come down and see you. Love will find a way, and all that."

"I ... I suppose so," said Becky despondently.

Jan made it all sound so simple, and Becky didn't think it was that simple at all. It wasn't just that she and Nick were going to be parted, it was that she seemed to be getting all the good luck, all the breaks, and he wasn't getting any. One of the things she'd always loved about Nick was that he didn't have any ego problems, or not compared to some guys, anyway. But now, she wasn't so sure.

How would I feel, she thought, if I'd failed all my exams and all my friends were getting jobs and going off to college and I wasn't? The thought made her shudder. I'd probably be every bit as fed up and moody as Nick is, she thought honestly. Especially if it meant losing the person I love...

"You've got to tell him, though," Jan went on.

"Just come right out with it; it's the only way. And tell him you'll come up and see him, and that he can come down to see you... Where are you going to live, by the way?"

"I'll probably stay at Mum's stepsister's. You remember Kate and Graham, don't you?" said Becky. "I stayed with them before. And then when I know my way around London a bit ... I suppose I'll share a flat... It was OK at their place, except that it's in Croydon, so it was rather a long way from the office."

"Where is the office?"

"Waterloo, not far from the station," said Becky enthusiastically. The two short weeks she'd spent in the magazine office in the summer had shown her a whole exciting new world, and it was one she longed to be part of.

"The building doesn't look like much, but once you get inside the offices are super, all potted plants and low Swedish-style furniture ... and computers, of course. It's all open-plan, so there's a really buzzy atmosphere, with phones ringing all the time and fax machines and messengers coming in with piles of clothes for the fashion department, or records for review..."

Jan began to laugh. "Now, that's more like it!" she said. "You actually sound excited, like someone who's just landed the job of their dreams. You've got to think about yourself, Becky, not just about how Nick's going to react to all this. You matter as well, you know. It's your job, your future. And if you and Nick aren't strong enough to cope with a little problem like this, well..."

"I wouldn't have said that Nick failing all his exams was a little problem, exactly!" Becky flared.

"I didn't meant that," said Jan. "I just meant that if you want it to work out between the two of you, if you *both* want it to work, then it will. In spite of everything. And in the meantime..."

"In the meantime...?" Becky prompted.

"I think you should look forward to going to London," Jan grinned. "I tell you, Becky, if it was me, my feet wouldn't touch the ground! Catch me staying in this dump a moment longer than I have to! As soon as I've got my secretarial diploma, I'm coming to London too. I want to work for a rich boss in travel or banking or something like that, with an office full of Swedish furniture and potted palms! And you and I, we'll share a penthouse flat with all those yuppies in Docklands, with a view over the River Thames, and loads of rich handsome guys fighting to take us out to dinner every night..."

"Oh Jan, you are an idiot," Becky said, but she couldn't help giggling, just the same.

I knew I'd feel better after I'd talked to Jan, she thought to herself after her friend had gone. It's all just going round and round in my head at the moment. She's right. I should be looking forward to going to London and starting my new job. This should be the most exciting time of my life. It's a new beginning, the beginning of my career as a journalist...

If only I didn't have to tell Nick!

"Becky?" her mum called up the stairs. "Becky, Kate's on the phone for you."

"All right, Mum, I'm coming." Becky ran downstairs and picked up the phone.

"Becky? Is that you? I hear you've got the job, you lucky thing," bubbled Kate, who was in her thirties and worked as a fashion buyer for one of the big London stores. "And we'll be seeing you in a couple of weeks, then?"

"Yes, that's right. They want me to start as soon as possible," said Becky, trying to sound more enthusiastic than she felt. She suspected that Kate would think she was a total wimp if she admitted that she was torn between the career of her dreams, and her love for Nick. As far as Kate was concerned, there was simply no contest. Women in the 1990s were expected to go for it. Becky was sure Kate loved her boyfriend, Graham, a gentle guy a couple of years younger than herself who worked as a freelance designer – but she couldn't imagine her ever letting him stand in the way of her career ambitions!

I wish I was like that, Becky thought. Or like Louise, who'd told her bluntly that she thought Nick's poor exam results were Nick's problem, not Becky's.

"Is your dad going to drive you down here?" Kate went on.

"He'll have to," Becky laughed. "I can't possibly manage all my stuff on the train! I think Mum's coming too; Mrs Piper next door said she'd have Emily for the day."

"It'll be a big change for your mum and dad, too, Becky," Kate said thoughtfully. "They'll miss you, you know."

"And I'll miss them," Becky admitted.

Later, in bed that night, she thought anxiously that it was quite true. Leaving home, starting a new job, a new life, was a big step. It had to happen, she knew that, but ... how would she get on in London, on her own?

OK, Kate would be there at first, but she couldn't stay in Kate and Graham's tiny spare room for ever. She'd be leaving her family, her friends, her home town, everything she knew. There'd be no Mum to wake her in the morning with a cup of tea and a gentle, "Up you get, Becky, it's school today." There'd be no Dad to pick her up from clubs and parties, or to slip a fiver into her hand for a minicab if she was going to be really late, with a murmured, "Take it, love. I want to be sure you get back safely." There'd be no Emily, gazing at her wide-eyed and eggy-faced across the breakfast table. No Jan living just round the corner. And no Nick...

Oh, help! Becky thought. What have I done? Supposing I hate it? Supposing I get homesick? Supposing I make a total mess of the job and get the sack? It was all very well making plans to conquer the world, but when you actually got that chance in a million, it was downright scary.

Especially when you had unfinished business left at home...

She sat up and tried to rearrange her crumpled duvet and pillows. I'll tell him the next time I see him, she thought. No use putting it off any longer. Jan's right: if he heard a rumour from anyone else it really would be awful. He'd never forgive me.

In the past, she and Nick had met, or talked on the phone, almost every day, but that was something else that had changed. Now three or four days sometimes went by without Becky hearing from him. As often as not, she ended up calling him, and, as her final weekend at home approached, that was what she did.

Jan and her cousin and some of their other friends were all meeting in the Rose and Crown on the Friday evening. If Nick and I meet a bit earlier, Becky thought, I can tell him about the job and then we can go on and have a night out with the others. Perhaps Jan was right, perhaps I am making a fuss about nothing. Perhaps Nick will be really pleased for me.

But however much she tried to reassure herself, there was a hard little knot of panic in the pit of her stomach when she thought about it. Oh, if only! she thought for about the thousandth time, as she picked up the phone to dial Nick's familiar number. If only he'd got into London University to do an engineering course, as we planned. If Nick was coming too…

But he wasn't, and there was nothing Becky could do about it.

"Hi! How are you?" she said when he came to the phone. She heard him yawn at the other end.

"OK, I s'pose. What have you been doing, then?"

"Not a lot. Jan came back from Crete; it sounds like she and Heather had a brilliant time. They're all meeting up in the Rose and Crown tonight; d'you fancy it? I thought we could maybe go for a pizza first, just the two of us. What d'you think?"

"If you like."

Even *talking* to Nick was hard work these days, Becky reflected. She could hear herself chattering mindlessly, making conversation, as if he was someone she'd only just met instead of her boyfriend.

"OK, then. Suppose we met at *Alfredo's* at half-past seven."

"Fine."

"Don't sound so keen!" Becky snapped, and then could have bitten her tongue out. She'd promised herself not to have a go at Nick, not while she knew how depressed he was. And here she was, yelling down the phone like an old nag.

"Sorry, I'm a bit tired," said Nick patiently. That made Becky feel even worse.

"See you later, then," she said.

That's it, she thought, as she put the phone down. There's no going back now. I've got an hour, an hour and a half, before we meet the others. That's plenty long enough to tell him, make plans...

But as she trailed upstairs, started running herself a hot bath and deciding what she was going to wear, she knew that she had never looked forward to anything less. It's make-or-break time, she thought grimly. Either Nick will swallow his pride, congratulate me, and start working out how we can go on seeing each other...

Or he won't.

And that could mean the end of the line for us...

2

"Nick, I..."

"Are you ready to order, signor? Signorina?"

A smiling waiter stood at Becky's elbow, his pad at the ready. Oh, no! Becky thought. As if this isn't difficult enough! She'd already tried to tell Nick once, but just at that moment a flashy, low-slung yellow sports car had driven by.

"Wow, look at that!" Nick had interrupted excitedly. "It must be a Ferrari, or even a Lamborghini. Someone must have won the Lottery; I've never seen one of those round here before. Sorry. You were saying?"

"It doesn't matter," said Becky.

Now, just as she had plucked up the courage to tell him again, the waiter had come to take their order.

"Quattro Stagioni for you, wasn't it, Becky?" Nick asked. "And I'll have ... umm ... the one with ham and mushrooms."

"*Si, signor*. Anything to drink?" said the waiter.

"Not for me, thanks," said Becky. The last thing I need is to feel all headachey and muzzy from drinking, she thought despairingly. Maybe this wasn't such a good idea, after all. I'm sure I won't be able to eat a thing.

Even her mum had advised her to tell Nick, as she was leaving the house to meet him. "The longer you leave it, the harder it will be," she had said sympathetically.

"I know," Becky groaned. "I shouldn't have kept putting it off, but he's been so touchy since the results came."

"I'm not surprised," said her mum, who liked Nick. "Everyone thought he'd pass, didn't they? Poor old Nick!"

Yes, poor old Nick, Becky thought guiltily. All the rest of their gang had done well enough. The only people who'd failed were real geeks and drop-outs like Johnny Lindsay and Luke Brittan – and Stephanie Hall who'd had rheumatic fever half-way through the year and hadn't expected to pass anyway. It hurt Becky deep inside to think of Nick being bracketed with them. He wasn't that type. And now she was going to make things worse by telling him that she had landed her dream job! If she ever got the chance...

She took a deep breath. "Nick," she said, "there's something I've got to tell you!"

She looked up and met his eyes. All at once his face took on a blank, shuttered expression, as if he was expecting bad news and was determined not to show any kind of emotional reaction.

"Oh, yes?" he said warily.

Why do things have to be so difficult? Becky thought. Why, oh why, couldn't Nick have passed his exams too, so that he could go off to college, make plans, join in with all the excitement? She closed her eyes.

"I've had a letter from Linda Hobson," she said.

"Linda Hobson?"

"You know, the Features Editor I worked for in July, in London."

"Oh, yes?" He wasn't making it any easier for her.

"She's offered me a job. A proper job. I mean, full-time. I … I'm going to work in London, Nick!"

He didn't say anything. After a moment that felt like a year, Becky looked at him. There was no expression on his face at all. In fact, he seemed to be avoiding her eyes.

"I see," he said. "When do you start?"

"Well, they want me as soon as I can get down there," Becky stammered. "It's … it's just a very junior job, Nick, more or less the same thing I was doing when I worked there in the summer – sorting the post, making coffee, learning how a magazine works, that kind of thing – but it's a wonderful opportunity, my big chance, really. You know I've always wanted to be a journalist…"

Her voice trailed away as she realized she was gabbling. Anything to fill up the awful, hurt silence. She peered up at Nick. He was gazing across the restaurant, his lips set in a firm line.

"Aren't … aren't you pleased for me, Nick?" she faltered. "Say something!"

He swung round to face her and she was

shocked at the bitterness in his voice as he said, "Congratulations!"

She caught at his arm but he shook her hand away. Becky's eyes filled with tears. This was worse, far worse than she had ever imagined. There was nothing she could say that would make Nick feel better. The plain fact was, she had a job, a future, and at the moment, he didn't. No wonder he sounded bitter. She'd have felt the same, in his place. But...

But he's supposed to love me, care about me, said a clear little voice in her head. Couldn't he even *pretend* to be pleased for me?

She tried again. "London's only an hour and a half away on the train," she pointed out. "I shall be coming home for weekends, Nick. It's not as though we won't be able to see each other. I mean, you could come down to London as well..."

Her voice trailed away. She could hardly bear to watch him, hunched into his old cord jacket, his untidy brown hair spilling down over the collar. How many times had she brushed that hair back from his face, run her fingers lovingly through it? But now...

Her breath caught on a sob.

"Oh, Nick, *please*," she whispered. "Don't ... don't be like that! I love you, you know I do! We'll work something out, I promise. We'll be able to see each other at weekends..."

"Weekends," Nick said flatly. "Oh, yes, that'll be great, won't it? Just great!"

"Well, it's better than nothing," said Becky, relieved that, at least, he seemed to be speaking to her again. Anything, even a full-scale row, was better than that oppressive, sulky silence. "And ... and we always knew there was a chance we wouldn't get into colleges where we could be together all the time! You said it didn't matter. You said we'd find a way to go on seeing each other, if we really wanted to. You said it would all work out..."

"I said a lot of things," said Nick moodily.

It's all over, Becky thought. He doesn't care any more. He can't, or he wouldn't be talking like this.

She felt a huge sob well up in her chest, and tried her hardest to choke it back. I can't cry here, in the middle of a restaurant, she thought. I'll have to go home, I'll have to ring Jan, I just can't handle this!

"Don't ... don't you want to see me any more?" she pleaded, hearing the pathetic, whining tone in her voice and hating herself. I should have more pride, she thought wretchedly, but this is Nick. I can't just let him go!

He made a little choked sound.

"Of course I still want to see you," he said. "You're the one who's going away, not me! I'm not going anywhere, remember? I shall be stuck here, trying to salvage something from the wreck of my so-called career plans, while you're swanning around in some glamorous job in London!

"How long d'you think we'll last, Becky? How long before you meet someone else, some character with pots of money and a fancy car, who can give you a much better time than I can?"

"But Nick," Becky faltered, "it's not like that!

I'm not like that! You know I'm not! If I wanted some rich guy with a flashy car there's plenty of them right here in town. It'll be the same in London!"

"No, it won't," said Nick bitterly. "In a couple of years you'll be too cool to bother with a small-town bloke like me. A small-town, unemployed bloke, what's more. You'll be turning your nose up at all of us, you wait and see. You'll get mixed up with a bunch of poncey media types called Dominic and Sebastian…"

Becky didn't know whether to laugh or cry. She shook her head.

"You've got it all wrong," she said. "It's not like that, honestly. Don't forget, I worked on the maga-zine in the summer. I know the people there. They're not 'poncey media types'; they're just ordinary people who happen to work on a magazine."

Nick shook his head stubbornly, and Becky began to feel annoyed.

"Is that what you think of me?" she demanded. "You think I'm some kind of shallow idiot with stars in her eyes who will forget her old mates and her home and the people she cares about just because she's got a job in London? I thought you knew me better than that, Nick!"

For almost the first time, she saw Nick hesitate, as if he wasn't as sure of himself as he pretended to be.

"I…" he began.

Just then, the waiter appeared with their order. Becky had never felt less like eating in her life.

"Black pepper, *bella signorina*?" said the waiter, brandishing an enormous pepper-mill. Normally, Becky thought the flirtatious attitude of the waiters was all part of the fun, but this time, she felt she could have picked up his pepper-mill and brained him with it. And Nick, too. How dare he assume she was a star-struck poser! Didn't he know her at all? Hadn't the last year of fun and friendship and love meant anything to him at all?

"No, thanks," she said brusquely, attacking her pizza in silence. She usually loved pizza, but this one tasted like cardboard.

Suddenly, Nick reached out across the table and took her hand.

"I'm sorry," he said awkwardly. "I didn't mean … it's just going to take a bit of getting used to, that's all."

He looked so sad that Becky's heart melted.

"I know," she said. "For me, too. But we can work something out, I know we can. As soon as I get settled, you'll have to come and see me."

"What with?" said Nick.

"What do you mean?"

"Aren't you forgetting something?"

"What?"

"I don't have any money," said Nick. "I haven't got a job, remember? And train fares don't come cheap."

"But I'll be earning," Becky began, and then wished she hadn't said anything. A closed, stubborn expression came over Nick's face, and they finished their meal in an unfriendly silence. This is awful, Becky thought. Whatever I say seems to be wrong…

She half-thought Nick would refuse to go and join the others in the pub, but when she suggested it, he shrugged and muttered, "OK, if you like."

When they went into the saloon bar of the Rose and Crown, Becky saw Jan, her cousin Rob and his girlfriend and a couple of their other friends at a corner table, laughing, joking, teasing each other, as if none of them had a care in the world. Nick and I used to be like that, Becky thought, with a pang of remembrance. It seemed ages since the two of them had had a really good time together, before exams and results and future plans had left a huge question mark hanging over their relationship. What's happened to us? Becky thought. It used to be so good...

"Hello, Nick. Hi, Becky," said Rob. "What are you drinking? It's my round. Shove up a bit, Jan, then Becky can sit next to you."

Becky squeezed in beside her friend, who raised her eyebrows questioningly. Becky nodded.

"You OK, mate?" Rob said to Nick. "You don't look..."

Becky felt a blush simmering up the back of her neck. She felt relieved when Nick spoke.

"It's all right," he said lightly, but there was a sarcastic edge to his voice that no one could miss. "Becky has just been telling me about her *brilliant* new job. It's in *London*, you know. On a *magazine*."

There was an embarrassed pause. No one knew quite what to say.

"That ... er ... that's great, Becky! Well done!" said Caroline, Rob's girlfriend, hurriedly.

"So you'll be leaving, then? Going to live in London, eh?" said one of the other guys.

Becky nodded. She couldn't look at Nick. This is a nightmare, she thought. An absolute nightmare. How could he humiliate me in front of all our friends?

Nick and Rob went up to the bar to get the drinks. Jan squeezed Becky's hand. "Want to talk about it?" she said sympathetically.

Becky shivered, although the evening was quite warm. "I ... I'm not sure what to say," she said bleakly.

"Well," said Jan, "at least he knows, now."

Becky nodded.

"And?"

"You heard him, Jan. It was awful," she said. "He ... he didn't even say well done, or that he was pleased for me, or anything. He just seems to think that I'm going to turn into some kind of London poser and that I won't have time for any of my old friends! Including him!"

"He's just jealous," said Jan calmly. "He'll get over it."

"But it's so unfair!" Becky cried. "I'm not like that! It's like he ... he doesn't trust me, or more like he doesn't know me, the kind of person I am. I'm not going to have my head turned by working on a magazine, truly I'm not."

"You'd better not, or I shall have something to say about it," Jan grinned.

Becky heaved a deep sigh.

"I don't know what I'm going to do, Jan," she said. "Nick and I, well, we go back a long way. I knew things would have to change once we'd all left school, but I thought Nick and I would stay together somehow. I thought that was what he wanted, too! At the very least, I thought we'd stay in touch, be friends. But now … it was like he hated me, like he didn't want to know! Like it was all over…"

At last, the tears came.

"I'm sure Nick didn't mean it like that," Jan said. "Don't cry, Becky."

"Yes, he did," Becky sobbed. "You should have heard him, going on about how I was bound to dump him for some media type called Dominic who drove a Ferrari!"

"You should be so lucky!" said Jan cheerfully. "I've told you, he's just jealous, and he's scared of losing you. Don't forget, this is a tough time for him. He's failed his exams, everyone else is going off to college or starting work. Then his girlfriend comes along and tells you she's landed her dream job…"

"But what was I supposed to do?" Becky demanded.

"You did the right thing. He'll come round, Becky. And if he doesn't…"

"If he doesn't, what?"

Jan winked at her. "There are plenty more fish in the sea!"

Becky mopped her eyes with a Kleenex provided by a puzzled Caroline, who was sitting at the other side of the table and watching them curiously.

Was Jan right? Becky thought. Would Nick come round, come to terms with the new situation? Or would their relationship be one of those that didn't survive all the changes that leaving school was bound to bring?

I thought Nick and I were so strong, Becky thought sadly, as she sipped her drink. I never thought he'd be like this! After all, it's not going to help his career prospects if I hang around here, getting nowhere, is it? One of us might as well go for it!

Nick and Rob and the other guys were engrossed in a conversation about cars, just as if nothing had happened. Caroline smiled at her.

"Nick's not keen on you going away, then?" she said.

Becky shook her head. She didn't know Caroline very well. She was the same age as Rob, a couple of years older than her and Jan.

"Men!" said Caroline with a sniff. "In spite of all the talk about equal rights, they really want us under their thumbs, don't they?"

"I didn't think Nick did," said Becky. "But things haven't been the same between us since he failed his A levels."

Caroline raised her eyebrows. "Tough one," she said. "You mean you passed, he failed?"

Becky nodded.

"Oh, don't worry too much," said Caroline. "I'm sure he'll come round – you've just got to give him time."

"That's what I keep telling her," put in Jan. "I'm sure when he's had time to get used to the idea, he'll be really pleased for you, Becky."

"But I don't *have* time," said Becky. "I'm going to London next week. Supposing ... just supposing

Nick and I haven't made it up by then?"

"You will have," said Jan confidently. "I'm sure you will. Nick won't want to risk losing you..."

When she got home that night, Becky sat despondently on the edge of her bed, wondering whether Jan and Caroline were right. Would Nick come round? Would he call her in a couple of days, as usual? She couldn't remember them ever having more than the most minor of tiffs before. Nick's easygoing nature was one of the things that had first attracted her to him. Some girls, she knew, went for mean, moody types, but not Becky. She and Nick had been friends for a long time before they started going out together. Now, Nick felt like a stranger.

He didn't telephone the next night. Or the night after that. Becky had plenty to do, sorting out the clothes and CDs and other belongings she wanted to take to London with her; seeing two friends off to university and another to the big teaching hospital where she was doing her training; shopping, talking to Jan... But still, there was something missing.

When four endless days had gone by with no call, she telephoned Jan, in tears.

"D'you think I should call him?" she wept. "I can't bear it to end like this, Jan! We haven't even said goodbye!"

"P'raps you'd better," Jan said. "Get it sorted out, once and for all. It's just male pride, you know, Becky. Nick's probably missing you every bit as much as you're missing him, only he doesn't want to admit it. Go on, give him a call. What have you got to lose?"

27

"That's true," said Becky. "Even if he tells me to get lost, I won't be any worse off than I am now!"

I can't believe this is happening, she thought to herself as she dialled Nick's number. Her palms were damp with sweat and her heart was beating wildly, just as if she and Nick hardly knew one another, hadn't shared all that laughter, all those kisses, all those moments of tenderness over the last, happy year. What was she going to say when he picked up the phone? And what would he say?

When she heard the phone being picked up her heart gave a colossal lurch and she nearly dropped the receiver.

"Hello?" came a familiar voice.

"Nick? It's Becky!" she breathed.

"Oh. Yes. Becky." He sounded embarrassed.

"Look, I think..." she began.

"Would you...?" he said, at exactly the same moment. Then they both began to laugh and Becky's spirits lifted. Perhaps it was going to be all right, after all.

"I'm sorry I haven't called," said Nick, sounding much more like his old self. "I've ... well, I've been thinking..."

"Yes?"

"Well ... oh, listen, we can't talk this over on the phone! How about meeting in the coffee lounge in the shopping centre tomorrow morning? About eleven?"

"OK, that's fine," said Becky, feeling very relieved. Perhaps Caroline and Jan were right, she thought. Perhaps all Nick needed was a bit of time to get used to the idea of me going away.

28

When they met in the shopping centre, Nick greeted her with a hug and a kiss. Becky breathed a sigh of relief. This was more like it, more like the easy, comfortable relationship that she and Nick had always had.

He bought coffee and Danish pastries and they managed to get seats at their special table in the corner. Becky felt a pang of nostalgia. We used to come here when we first started going out together, she thought. We used to sit here for ages, just holding hands and gazing into each other's eyes, making a cup of coffee or a Coke last hours, hoping that the waitresses wouldn't throw us out. Does Nick remember those times, too? Is that why he brought me here?

Suddenly, Nick spoke. "I've been a creep," he said, stirring his coffee thoughtfully.

Becky didn't reply.

"I shouldn't have had a go at you about your job," he said, grabbing her hand. "It's good news for you, of course it is. It's just…"

"I do understand, you know," Becky said gently. "It was really bad luck, you not getting your exams, Nick!"

"Or maybe it wasn't," he said. "Maybe I'm just not up to it!"

"Oh, Nick, don't say that! You are!" Becky cried eagerly. "I know you are! This is just a setback, that's all. You could do re-sits, or maybe think about getting a job … or I was reading in the paper not long ago about grants for young people who wanted to set up their own businesses. Wouldn't you like that, being your own boss?"

Nick shrugged.

"Well, maybe," he said. "The trouble is, Becky, I don't really know what I want to do. If I did, I'd do it! I only really applied for college because everyone else was and the careers adviser and my year tutor expected me to."

Becky just looked at him, realizing that what he had said was true. Nick had never been as ambitious as she was.

But that needn't affect us, Nick and me. Need it? she thought.

"I ... I'm sorry, Becky," Nick was saying. "I can't help it, I don't want you to go away! I know you said we could see each other at weekends..."

"But we can!" said Becky. "I'll come up, you can come down. Maybe you could even get a job in London."

"Oh, yeah? What as?" said Nick. "Besides, I don't want to live in London. I like it here. My mates are here, the lads from the football team. What's London got that you can't get here, and about half the price?"

Becky gave up. He just can't see it, she thought. I've lived here for seventeen, nearly eighteen years and it's time to move on! There's a whole big, wide world out there – new people, new places, new opportunities.

Don't ask me to give that up, Nick, she pleaded silently. I couldn't do it. I *do* love you, but...

"We'll work something out," she said hopefully. Even as the words left her mouth, she wondered whether they were true.

"I ... I love you, Becky," Nick murmured.

Becky felt a lump appear in her throat. Nick wasn't the demonstrative type. A quick hug, an arm round her shoulders, a squeeze of her hand was more his style. He didn't go in for romantic declarations, as a rule. She could practically count the times he'd told her he loved her on the fingers of one hand. And now, here he was, telling her how much she meant to him just as she was about to leave him!

She swallowed hard. Why did life have to be so difficult? It would've been easy, or at least easier, to leave the cold, unfriendly stranger Nick had become after the results came. But this Nick, sad-eyed and pleading, how could she bear to say goodbye to him?

She tried to think about the magazine, about Linda and the other girls, about the wonderful new career stretching out in front of her. What's the use of having a fantastic future if I'm leaving my heart behind? she thought bleakly.

"You're really dead set on going, then?" Nick said.

Becky closed her eyes. Am I? she thought.

Then, very slowly, she nodded. "I'm sorry, Nick," she said.

Nick got up, pushing his chair back so abruptly that it nearly fell over.

"I suppose I can't blame you," he said coldly. "What is there to keep you here, after all? Only a jobless, useless failure like me!"

"Nick, you're not..." Becky called after him.

But he had gone.

3

The night before Becky left for London, Jan came round to say goodbye. She'd bought a box of chocolates and home-made "Good Luck" card featuring a cartoon-style Becky sitting behind an enormous desk marked "Editor", smoking a fat cigar and bellowing, "Hold the front page!" Becky giggled, but there was a lump in her throat as she hugged her friend.

"Oh, Jan," she said in a choked voice, "I'm going to miss you!"

Jan nodded. "It's really weird being here now that Suzanne and the others have gone. Felicity will be off if she gets her Oxford scholarship, and now you!"

"Everything's going to be different from now on," Becky sighed. "It's not that I'm having second thoughts, but ... oh, I don't know. Suppose I don't like it? Suppose I make a complete mess of the whole thing?"

Jan squeezed her hand reassuringly. "You won't. You'll be brilliant; I know you will!"

"Thanks, Jan!"

In spite of what Jan had said, Becky found it hard to get to sleep that night. Her little bedroom, with the blue-and-white wallpaper that had faded in places and still showed the marks of her old pop posters, suddenly seemed very comfortable and homely and, well, safe. Kate and Graham's spare room just wouldn't be the same. And how would she get on in a flat, sharing with other girls, cooking her own meals, budgeting for everything from gas bills to loo rolls? And would she *really* be any good as a journalist, when she'd progressed from washing the coffee mugs and sorting the post to real writing? Would she ever get to do any real writing?

She sat up, noticing that the clock said half-past twelve. I hope I've done the right thing, she thought. Maybe I'm not ready to strike out on my own. Maybe Nick was right and I'll end up as some kind of awful snob, turning my nose up at my old friends and my family...

She hadn't spoken to Nick again since the disastrous meeting in the shopping centre. She had waited, the next day, for him to call, and when he didn't, she had swallowed her pride and called him. I can't just go off to London without even saying goodbye, she thought forlornly. Even if he doesn't want to see me any more. I've got to say goodbye to him, at least...

But when she called his house, he wasn't there. She left a message with his older brother, but he didn't call back, even though she sat by the phone all evening. That's it, she thought bleakly. It's all over.

It was hard to believe. Losing Nick was going to leave a huge, aching gap in her life…

She turned over again and buried her face in her pillow. What am I going to do? she thought. No Nick, London, a new job, it's all too much.

"One thing at a time, Becky!"

Her mum's advice came back to her. Mum and Dad believe in me, she thought, and so does Jan. Maybe they're right. Anyway, I can't sort it all out tonight, or even tomorrow. I'll just have to see how it goes. Take it a day at a time…

The thought was faintly comforting as she drifted off to sleep.

The next morning was chaos. Becky felt tired and headachey after her bad night. There seemed to be more cases and boxes and bags to be squeezed into her dad's car than any one person could possibly need. Emily, who was being left at home with the next-door neighbour as babysitter, was unusually bad-tempered and fractious.

"I want to come! Want to come wiv you!" she wailed for about the twentieth time. Becky picked her up.

"You can't, darling," she explained patiently. "It's ever such a long way in the car and you know you hate it."

"No!" yelled Emily, wriggling and stiffening so that Becky nearly dropped her. "Want to come! WANT TO COME!"

"Here, I'll take her, Becky," smiled Mrs Piper, reaching out her arms to the squirming, kicking toddler.

Becky ran upstairs again to check that she

hadn't left anything behind. Her bedroom looked bare and forlorn. No clothes strewn around, no dressing-gown hanging on the back of the door, no clock or photos beside her bed: it looked like a guest-room. Becky felt tears pricking the back of her eyes.

"Becky?" her mother's voice called.

Becky gave a huge sniff and yelled, "Coming!"

"Becky, Nick's here!"

Her heart leapt into her throat. Nick! What did he want? She walked down the stairs on trembling legs. Her parents seemed to have tactfully disappeared and Nick stood in the middle of the front room, looking nervous.

"Becky, I…" he began.

She stared at him without a word.

"I … couldn't let you go without saying goodbye," he stammered, thrusting a bunch of freesias into her hand. "I … I'm sorry, Becky. I … I do wish you the best of luck, honestly I do! I … I know I should've called."

"Oh, Nick…"

Becky stepped forward uncertainly. Then, suddenly, she was in his arms and it was just like old times.

"I'll write to you!" Becky gasped. "And … and I'll call you, and I'm sure I'll be coming home for a weekend quite soon!"

He nodded.

Becky heard her father come into the hall, clearing his throat noisily.

"Goodbye, Nick!" she said, looking up into his warm brown eyes, trying to impress every one of his features on her memory: the scattering of freckles on the bridge of his nose, the odd little twist of his eyebrows, the firm line of his jaw... Oh, she was going to miss him so much! He kissed her; a warm, familiar, loving kiss that reminded her of the hundreds of other kisses they had shared over the months they'd been together. How can I bear to leave him? Becky thought. I must be crazy...

For one mad, wild moment she thought of telling Nick, telling everyone, that it was all a mistake, that she didn't want to go to London after all. Then, as she and Nick broke apart, she saw her dad in the doorway, smiling at them ... her handbag and coat in the hall ... her mum, waiting in the car that was already piled with her possessions. She thought of Linda and the others at the magazine office, where she would be joining them on Monday morning, and experienced a little quiver of excitement.

"Goodbye, Nick," she said softly. "I'll call you as soon as I can, and I'll write to you as soon as I've settled in!"

Then, still clutching the bunch of freesias, she followed her father out to the car.

Staying with Kate and Graham felt like a rather peculiar holiday, Becky told herself some hours later, as she tried to fit her clothes into the tiny spare-room wardrobe. She put the photos of her parents and Emily, Nick and the Sixth Form gang on the bedside table, to help herself feel more at home. Already, her old life seemed a long way away. I'm a London working girl now, she told herself.

It still didn't feel quite real.

"Becky? Dad and I are going to have to make a move, love. We don't want to be home too late," came her mother's voice.

Becky swallowed hard. I'm not a baby any more, she thought. I'm seventeen, nearly eighteen. I should be able to say goodbye to my parents without howling as if I was Emily's age!

All the same, it was a strange feeling watching her dad's car disappearing around the corner of Kate's street, her mum's hand waving out of the window until she couldn't see it any more.

"OK, Becky?" said Kate. "I bet you're excited, aren't you? Talk about the opportunity of a lifetime! Jobs on magazines are like gold dust, you know. What did your friends at home say when you told them?"

"Well, Jan – she's my best friend – was really pleased for me," said Becky. "And Louise, my other friend, she's gone off to Australia with her family."

"What about what's-his-name? Nick?"

Becky bit her lip, not knowing quite what to say.

"Oh, like that, is it?" said Kate understandingly. "Didn't he want you to go away? Was that it? You mustn't let him hold you back, Becky…"

"Oh, it's not just that," said Becky. She suddenly felt so tired that all she wanted to do was curl up with Kate's huge, comforting tabby cat Charlie Boy and go to sleep. "It's … you see, the thing is, Kate, we'd planned to go to London together. Not necessarily to the same college, but at least the same city! But then, Nick failed his A levels…"

"But why? What happened? Didn't he do any work?"

Becky shook her head. "I … I don't know. I don't think it was that. He said, the other day, that he'd only applied to college because everyone expected him to. He's … well, he's just not very ambitious…"

"Not like you," said Kate.

"I … I suppose not…"

Kate got up from where she'd been sitting on the sofa and came and knelt on the floor beside Becky.

"Look," she said, "I don't want to sound hard, but you're only young, Becky. If Nick's the right one for you, if it's meant to last, then it will, no matter what. And if it's not, if you've grown out of the relationship, grown apart, well, there are plenty of other nice guys out there."

Becky nodded, not quite trusting herself to speak.

"I know," she said. "It's lovely to be here with you, Kate," she added hastily, as the big, fluffy tabby wound himself round her legs, purring. "But I can't help wondering how this job's going to turn out…"

"It's going to turn out wonderfully," said Kate firmly. "They must have been impressed with you, or they wouldn't have taken you on full-time. You've got nothing to worry about. Now, would you like a cup of tea? Or something stronger, since this is a bit of a celebration?"

"Tea would be fine, thanks," said Becky.

When she woke up the next morning, Becky

couldn't think where she was. Then she remembered, it was her first day at work! She was halfway out of bed before it occurred to her to look at her watch. It was twenty-past six! Feeling rather silly, she crept back under the sheets and blankets, shivering with nerves. This is it, she thought. My first day as a real journalist. Well, sort of...

When she went downstairs, Kate had already left for work, but Graham sat at the kitchen table, tucking into bacon and eggs. Even the smell made Becky's stomach churn.

"Like some? There's plenty," he offered cheerfully, but Becky shook her head. It was as much as she could do to choke down a slice of toast and a cup of tea. Graham raised one eyebrow.

"Nervous, are you?" he said kindly, buttering another slice of toast.

Becky nodded.

"Don't worry, Becky. By the end of this week, you'll be feeling quite at home, you wait and see!"

Becky hoped he was right.

It didn't help when the train she'd caught with time to spare stopped, for no reason, in the middle of nowhere. Becky was jammed in with all the other hot, fidgety commuters, most of whom seemed to have brought newspapers or books to read. Nobody spoke.

Oh, no! Becky thought. That's all I need. I don't want to be late on my very first morning! Whatever will Linda think?

Eventually the train began to move again. When Becky got off she ran all the way to the office, arriving on the doorstep, flushed and panting, at about a minute to ten. She was in such a rush that she almost tripped and fell over the threshold.

"Whoops!" said the security guard.

"Someone's in a hurry," added a male voice with an American accent, slipping an arm under Becky's to steady her. She felt embarrassment prickle up the back of her spine. Surely it couldn't be ... but yes, it was, Harvey Preston, the Managing Director and owner of the company, whom Linda had pointed out to her in the summer! Becky felt as though she wanted to curl up and die on the spot.

"I ... I'm sorry!" she gasped, scarlet in the face from a combination of running and sheer embarrassment.

But Mr Preston was smiling in a friendly way.

"No need to apologize," he said. "I like to think my staff are in a hurry to get to work on a Monday morning!"

Then he frowned. "You do work here, don't you?" he said. "I don't seem to have seen you before, or have I?"

Almost too shy to speak, Becky managed to stammer, "No. Well, yes ... I'm new, but I did work here for a couple of weeks in the summer..."

"Oh, yes," said Mr Preston, "I remember, you're Linda's assistant, the Work Experience girl!"

He beamed at her and held out his hand.

"Welcome to Preston Publications," he said. "I hope you'll be happy with us!"

"Th-thank you. I'm Becky Rivers," said Becky.

"Nice to have you on board, Becky!"

Becky breathed a sigh of relief as the lift travelled slowly upwards. Falling over the boss wasn't exactly the best start to her new job, but he'd been very nice and friendly, and at least he knew who she was.

She went into the magazine offices on the second floor and headed straight for Linda's desk, where she'd worked before. There didn't seem to be anyone around. Feeling like a spare part, Becky stood by the desk and waited. After a few moments, a red-haired girl wearing black leggings and a baggy T-shirt came in, dumped a pile of post on Linda's desk, and smiled at Becky.

"Hi," she said. "I'm Fiona Bedford, the Editor's secretary."

"I'm Becky Rivers. I start work today."

"Oh, yes." Fiona's brow cleared. "Nice to meet you, Becky. You came in when I was on holiday, didn't you? And did a great job, from what I heard!"

Becky blushed, warmed by this friendly welcome.

"Linda will be in very soon, I'm sure," Fiona went on. "In the meantime, why don't you make yourself a cuppa? Linda likes a black coffee as soon as she gets in. You know where everything is, don't you?"

She indicated the corner where the coffee, tea, sugar and mugs were kept on top of an ancient fridge which – if you were lucky – held fresh milk. Becky grinned suddenly. She'd said she didn't mind starting as the office tea-girl and it looked as though that was what she was doing!

By the time Linda arrived, Becky had washed up four mugs and seven teaspoons, wiped the tray and the top of the fridge, and filled the kettle in the cloakroom down the corridor.

"Hi, Becky! Your first day as a magazine journalist-to-be, eh? How does it feel?" Linda said.

"Great!" said Becky truthfully. If everyone from the Editor's secretary to her own boss to the Managing Director of the company seemed pleased that she was part of the team, how could she help feeling good?

"Would you like a coffee?" she offered. "The kettle's just boiled."

Linda burst out laughing.

"I can tell you're going to be an asset to the magazine," she said cheerfully. "Someone to make me my first cup of coffee of the morning, that's what I need."

Becky soon realized that working on the magazine full-time was going to be different from her summer job. Then, she had just filled in where she was needed. Now, Linda made certain that she knew what her duties were.

"You know that we're the Features Department, of course," she said as she sipped her coffee. "There's me, Sandie and Paula, who are our staff writers, and yourself. We're responsible for all the articles in the magazine that aren't fashion or beauty. Lisa is our Fashion Editor, and Melissa, who's a freelancer, deals with beauty and health. Liz Mackenzie is our problem-page lady. She's freelance too, but the letters come to us and we send them on to her. Every week we have a news page to edit, the readers' letters, a couple of real-life stories, one or two pop or film-star interviews, and an 'emotional'."

Becky must have looked blank, because Linda went on, "Our 'emotional' is an article on an emotional subject like ... well, it could be living in a step-family, or being a teenage mum, or saying no to sex. Some of our emotionals are written in-house, by Sandie or Paula, but others are sent in by freelancers, mostly regulars we know we can rely on. Oh, and we have a careers page, and film, record and book reviews, and our 'Guy's Look at Life' which is written by Guy Middleton, another freelancer..."

Becky's head was reeling by then.

"It does seem a lot," she said faintly.

Linda grinned. "Well, that's why we need you," she said. "Generally things work quite smoothly but we do have the odd panic when a feature comes in late or an interview is cancelled."

"What happens then?" Becky wanted to know.

"Use something from stock. Or we can ring one of the freelancers, or do a quick cuttings job."

Becky felt very ignorant. "What's a cuttings job?" she said.

"A cuttings job is an article on a star which is written without meeting them, just by going through old press cuttings. It's much nicer to get an exclusive interview, of course, but that's just not possible every time."

"I remember wondering whether journalists really, truly met all the stars they wrote about," replied Becky thoughtfully.

"Well, now you know," Linda replied. "Sometimes they do, sometimes they don't." She drained her coffee.

"Right," she said, "time to get going. Becky, will you open and sort the post, please?"

She handed Becky an enormous pile of envelopes both large and small and pointed to a desk in the corner, next to Paula, one of the writers, who was hard at work at her computer keyboard.

"That'll be your desk, Becky, OK?"

"Yes. Thanks," said Becky. Her brain still seemed to be reeling from all the information she'd been given. Was Melissa the Beauty Editor or the problem-page lady? Where should she file readers' letters? What went on the news page? It was all more than frightening, it was terrifying. How would she ever remember it all? Oh, well, she thought, as she looked at the pile of post. I'd better make a start...

She was just "filing" a brochure about a new range of gas fires into the waste paper basket when the telephone rang, nearly making her jump out of her skin. She picked up the receiver.

"Hello?" she said cautiously.

"Could I speak to Becky Rivers, please?" came a familiar voice.

"Jan!" Becky squealed. "It's me! Where are you? What are you doing?"

"I'm at college, silly. Just thought I'd ring and wish you luck!" said Jan. "We're having a coffee break and I've only got one 20p, so you'd better talk fast! Is everything all right?"

"Yes. Well, I think so," said Becky. "I've got here, at least! I fell over the boss on my way in, but he didn't seem to mind. Linda's just given me the post to sort…" The pips went.

"Got to go," said Jan. "Ring me up soon, or write me a nice long letter, OK?"

"I will," said Becky, just before the phone went dead.

Nice of Jan to call, she thought, trying not to wish that the call had been from Nick. Still, guys don't think of things like that. And he did bring me flowers, and wish me luck … was it only yesterday morning? It seemed a lifetime ago. Perhaps he'll call me this evening.

Paula, at the next desk, suddenly leaned back in her chair and smiled at Becky.

"Hi," she said. "Sorry I haven't had time to chat but this copy's due to go to the printers and the art room are screaming for it! Hang on a mo while I print it out, then we can relax a bit."

Becky had met Paula during the summer, but not Sandie, the other writer, who had just joined the magazine. There was no sign of Sandie this morning and Becky wondered where she was. As if she could read her thoughts, Paula said, "Sandie's out today, doing an interview."

"Anyone nice?" Becky asked.

"It's that bloke who's just joined the cast of *EastEnders*."

Perhaps I'll be doing that one day, thought Becky longingly. Interviewing hunky actors, instead of making the coffee and sorting the post!

She had never known a morning pass so quickly.

Fiona, the Editor's secretary, asked her to join her and two of the sub-editors for lunch in a local sandwich bar by the river.

"What do you think of it so far?" she asked Becky with a grin.

"Er…" Becky began. "Quite honestly, I don't know whether I'm on my head or my heels at the moment. There seems to be so much to remember."

"That first-day feeling. I remember it well!" groaned Aisha, one of the subs. "Don't worry, Becky, you'll get use to it. Where did you work before?"

"I didn't," Becky admitted shyly. "This is my first job."

"Oh, wow!" laughed Fiona. "Where are you from, Becky? Are you still living at home?"

Becky shook her head. "No, I'm staying with my mum's stepsister in Croydon for the time being. I shall start looking for a flat once I know my way around London a bit, though. Kate's lovely, but her spare room's not very big, and besides, I feel like a gooseberry with her and her fella."

Fiona looked at her thoughtfully. "One of my flatmates is moving out in a couple of weeks," she said. "Our place is in Camberwell. It's nothing special as flats go, but it's on a bus route. You could come and have a look at it sometime if you like."

Becky felt herself blushing, warmed by Fiona's friendliness. After all, she hardly knew her, and here she was, suggesting she might like to move into her flat!

"That's very kind of you," she said shyly.

"Not kind at all. We need someone to share the rent, and you don't look like you have too many anti-social habits!" Fiona laughed.

Then Aisha looked at her watch. "Come on, you lot," she commanded. "It's almost two. Time to get back."

Becky returned to the office in good spirits. For the first time in days, she actually felt relaxed. It's all going to work out, she thought optimistically. The job, living in London, Nick – I'm going to work it out!

Later in the afternoon, Linda asked her to make teas all round. She walked down the corridor, balancing a tray loaded with full mugs, and nudged open the swing doors with her foot.

"Look where you're going, you idiot!" came a furious voice.

Becky gasped, lost her grip on the tray, and the mugs slithered to the ground, drenching the slim, blonde girl behind the door in hot tea.

She squealed, and began dabbing at her cream-coloured mac with a tissue.

"I'm terribly sorry," Becky murmured, scarlet with mortification, "I didn't see … oh, no, your coat… Look, would you like me to take it and soak it in the sink straight away? I can't tell you how sorry I am…"

Fiona and Linda, disturbed by the commotion, had come out to see what was going on.

"Are you OK, Sandie? What happened?" said Linda.

"Yes, I'm OK, no thanks to this … this clown," snapped Sandie.

Becky was almost in tears. "I'm so sorry," she faltered, "it was an accident…"

Linda glanced at her scarlet cheeks and trembling mouth and gave her a reassuring smile.

"Of course it was," she said soothingly. "And there's no real harm done. You're not scalded, are you? Let Becky go and soak your coat for you."

"Becky?" snarled the blonde girl.

"Yes. This Becky Rivers, our new Features junior. Becky, this is Sandie Johnson, our other writer."

"Hello," said Becky. "I … I'm really sorry about your coat, Sandie."

Sandie didn't reply. Her grey eyes were like chips of ice, and she looked at Becky with real dislike. She looks as if she hates me, Becky thought in dismay. But why? Anyone can make a mistake, and I did say I was sorry.

Sandie swept away without another word, leaving Becky gazing after her. With a sinking heart, she realized that her dream job was going to have its "down" side, after all. And the down side looked remarkably like Sandie Johnson…

4

"**D**ear Nick, Thanks for your letter."
Becky chewed the end of her Biro thoughtfully. She wouldn't have believed it would be so hard to write a letter to Nick. Nick, of all people! The trouble is, she thought miserably, if I go on about work and what fun it is, it sounds as though I'm showing off, rubbing it in that I'm having a better time than he is. But what else can I tell him? She picked up Nick's letter again. If you can call it a letter, she thought gloomily. A couple of sides of scribble, that mostly seemed to be about football. He didn't even say he missed me! Oh, well...

"I can't believe I've been working in London for a whole month already!" she wrote. "Except, I got my first pay packet the other day. I think I'll frame it – the pay packet, I mean, not the money. Most of that's gone already. Living here is very expensive! I had to buy a monthly season ticket as I'm not sure how long I'll go on living with Kate and Graham. Fiona, one of the girls at work, (I told you about her, didn't I? Long red hair, really friendly, she's the Ed's secretary) lives in a shared flat in Camberwell. One of her flatmates is moving out in a couple of weeks and Fi says I might be able to move in, if the others agree.

"I've had an idea. If I do move into the flat, why don't you come down and help me move? Steve would let you borrow his van, just this once, wouldn't he? Then you could stay the weekend, meet Fi and the others; it'd be great. I do miss you, you know.

"I still love the job. I wrote my first bit of 'copy' today! (That's what they call it.) It was a description of a new alarm-clock for our news page. Linda said it was fine, though Sandie was sniffy, as usual. She really seems to have it in for me. I was worried about it until Fi told me that she, Sandie that is, has a younger sister she wanted to get my job! Tough! Luckily, she goes out quite a lot doing interviews. When she's in, she just ignores me. I've tried to stay on the right side of her and keep out of her way as much as I can. It didn't help that I spilled a cup of tea over her the first time we met. The way she carried on, you'd have thought I did it on purpose."

Becky put her pen down. What else can I tell him? she thought. When she wrote to Jan, there always seemed to be so much to say that her hand started to ache. Writing to Nick was a real struggle. But then, Jan's own letters were always crammed with bits of gossip from home, and all the news she wanted to hear. Much as she loved her new job and her new life, Becky always felt a pang of homesickness when Jan's letters came.

"I saw Nick the other day," Jan had written in the last one. "He looked dead miserable. I asked him if he'd heard from you and he just said he had and mooched off!"

Of course Nick's heard from me, Becky thought crossly. When she first wrote, she had enclosed Kate and Graham's phone number, just in case he'd lost it, but Nick hardly ever called. One evening, when she'd been feeling especially lonely, she'd plucked up the courage to call him instead.

"Nick? It's Becky!"

"Oh, hi, Becky!"

Becky felt snubbed. Was he pleased she'd rung, glad to hear from her, or not? "Well ... er ... how are you? How's it going?"

"OK. Well, there's nothing much happening. You know what this place is like."

Silence.

God, this is awful, Becky thought. You wouldn't think that Nick was supposed to be my boyfriend, that we'd been together for all those months. Tears prickled the back of her eyes. What was the matter with him? Wasn't he even interested in how she was getting on? Didn't he miss her at all?

"How's the job, then?" he said, after an embarrassingly long pause.

"Great! I mean, well, I really like it, you know?" Becky gabbled. Oh, dear, she thought, I don't want to sound as though I'm gloating because I've got a job and he hasn't. I know it must be hard for him...

"Everyone's really friendly," she went on, trying not to think of Sandie Johnson's icy stares and sneering manner. "I don't do anything exciting, only open and file post and check addresses and phone numbers and things like that. I ... I'm sure I'll be coming home for the weekend soon," she finished guiltily.

"That'll be nice," said Nick. Was he being sarcastic, or just polite? It was hard to tell ... and he certainly didn't sound as though he was counting the days till he saw her again.

What can I do? Becky thought. Nick's never been good on the phone, he never had to be. At home, we mostly just said, "See you at Puzzles!" or, "Meet you round at Rob's!"

"Look, I've got to go," she said hastily. "I don't want to run up a huge bill on Kate's phone. I'll see you soon, OK? And ... and Nick..."

"Mmm?"

He sounded so bored that Becky's "I love you" stuck in her throat. Instead, she just said, "Nice to talk to you. Take care!" and put the phone down, feeling depressed. I wish I hadn't called him, she thought.

"Did you get through to Nick? How was he?" said Kate as she went gloomily into the living-room.

"Yes, I did. He sounded fed up," said Becky briefly.

Kate raised one eyebrow.

"Oh, those male egos," she said with a grin. "There are too many guys like that, Becky. They want us women rushing round, paying them attention, and they feel threatened if a woman has a life and career of her own!"

"Present company excepted, I hope!" said Graham, looking up from the magazine he was reading.

"Of course. You're one in a million, aren't you, love?" said Kate affectionately.

Becky felt a lump in her throat as she caught the loving glance they exchanged. It *can* work out, sometimes, she thought enviously. Kate's a lot more successful than Graham, and I think she earns more too, but he never seems to mind.

"Don't let him push you around, Becky," Kate advised. "What does he do, by the way?"

Becky flopped into an armchair with a sigh.

"That's the trouble," she said. "He isn't doing anything. Since he failed his exams he seems to have lost motivation... He doesn't seem to want to do anything..."

"And you got your job and came down here, and he was left behind," said Graham sympathetically. "It can't have been easy for him, Becky. Especially if he can't get a job."

"Oh, I know. I understand that. But ... he's just been so moody and miserable, I don't know what to say to him any more," said Becky. "He's changed. When I talked to him on the phone just now, we didn't seem to have anything to say to each other."

Kate nodded. "How long have you known him?"

"Oh, ages. We were at school together, then we started going out about this time last year. We had a lot of fun. He's a lovely guy, or at least he was..."

"And do you think it might be time to finish it?" Kate asked bluntly.

Becky was silent for a moment. Finish with Nick? She couldn't! Could she? She thought of the fun they'd had, the happiness they'd shared ... and Nick's warning when she first told him about her new job. He'd been so sure she wouldn't want to know him any more.

If she finished with him now, it would prove he was right!

One thing, Becky thought as she slipped Nick's letter into the pillar-box on her way to the station next morning, there's too much to do at work for me to sit around, thinking about Nick! I *do* miss him, and the way we used to be, but I've got so much else to think about. So much to learn...

She was in the office before any of the others that morning, so she made herself a coffee and started to go through the daily papers. She was just reading a story about a Scottish schoolgirl who had saved her two young brothers from a burning house when one of the phones rang.

"Hello, Features Department?" she said.

"Could I speak to Sandie Johnson, please?"

"I'm sorry, she's not ... er ... she's not here at the moment," said Becky politely. Sandie had already had a go at her for saying. "She's not in yet!" in reply to an early-morning call – even though it was perfectly true! "May I take a message?"

"It's about her interview this afternoon. I'm afraid we're going to have to postpone it; the band's flight has been delayed. If Sandie calls me, I'll give her all the details."

"OK," said Becky, scribbling on a Post-It note. "Who's calling, please?"

"Vicky Bray, Cresta Records Press Office."

"Does Sandie have your number?"

"Yes, she does."

"OK. I'll tell her."

Becky stuck the Post-It note to Sandie's computer screen. Just then, Linda came in. "Morning, Becky. How are things?"

"Fine," said Becky. "I'll get your coffee… Oh, and there's a really good story in one of the tabloids about a girl in Scotland who saved her two little brothers from a fire. Here, I cut it out for you."

Linda glanced at the cutting. "Sounds interesting. Pass it to Paula when she comes in, would you, Becky? We could do a follow-up story."

Becky nodded, wondering how long it would be before she got the chance to write a story herself, rather than handing it over to Paula or Sandie. Writing about new alarm-clocks and putting the readers' letters page together was all very well, but she was dying to have a go at some real writing!

"Has Liz McKenzie's problem page come in yet, Becky?" Linda asked.

"I'm not sure," Becky admitted. "I haven't had a chance to go through the post yet."

"She might have faxed it through last night. It was due yesterday, but one of her kids was ill and she got delayed," the Features Editor went on, rummaging among the pile of papers on her desk. "Oh, yes, here it is, she did fax it, bless her. You'd better key it into the system, Becky. Liz's file is on our network. You know how to do it, don't you?"

Becky nodded, taking the faxed pages from Linda, sitting down at her own screen, and switching on. Dealing with the problem page took up most of the morning. At lunchtime Fiona, who was universally known as Fi, put her head round the door and said, "Fancy a sandwich by the river, Becky?"

"Just let me finish the problem page," said Becky, pressing the SAVE key.

"About the flat," Fi said as the two girls sat down to eat their sandwiches. "Lorraine's moving in with her boyfriend in a couple of weeks, so we are going to need a fourth person. I told Ruth and Jade about you, and they want to meet you. Oh, don't worry," she added, as Becky looked alarmed, "they'll like you OK. They're ever so easy going – well, we all are! And I told them you don't have any horrible habits as far as I know!"

Becky giggled. "Thanks, Fi," she said gratefully, "it's really good of you. It's OK living at Kate's, but I do get fed up with the travelling..."

"And I don't suppose the night life's up to much either," said Fi with a sympathetic grin. "OK, Becky. Come home with me tomorrow night and have supper and see what you think. The rent's cheapish, and we have a kitty for things like bread and milk and loo rolls. And it's only a bus ride from here!"

Still chatting, the two girls made their way back to the office via the craft shops and trendy restaurants of Gabriel's Wharf. Becky was just scrolling through the problem-page letters again, making sure she hadn't left anything out, when

Sandie Johnson erupted into the room, flinging her coat and bag down on a chair. She looked furious.

"Whatever's the matter?" asked Paula mildly.

"Rock bands!" snapped Sandie bad-temperedly. "I've just trailed half-way across London to interview Apocalypse and the hotel receptionist told me they're not due to check in until six this evening! I tried to ring the record company to find out what had happened, but Vicky was out at lunch. What a waste of time!"

A band of ice seemed to have settled around Becky's heart. Vicky, she thought. Vicky from Cresta Records... Oh, no!

She turned round, scarlet in the face from embarrassment. "Er ... Sandie," she stammered. "There ... there was a message for you this morning from Vicky Bray from Cresta Records, saying your interview would have to be postponed..."

Sandie shot her a look of the purest venom. "Oh, there was, was there?" she sneered sarcastically. "Where is this message, then?"

Wordlessly, Becky pointed to Sandie's computer screen, where the yellow Post-it note still fluttered.

"Oh, great," said Sandie. "Didn't you notice I wasn't in this morning, you stupid ... little girl? I had a dental appointment, and then I was going straight over to Kensington to do my interview!"

"I ... I didn't know," faltered Becky.

"Didn't it even occur to you that the message was urgent?" raged Sandie. "Linda's got the number of my mobile phone. You could have saved me a wasted journey, you dummy!"

"I ... I," Becky stammered, not knowing what to say. It was true, she hadn't really noticed that Sandie wasn't there. She was out so often, and Becky had been so busy anyway, that the message from the record company had gone right out of her head.

"I suppose that's what comes of employing amateurs," Sandie snapped. "I'll ring Vicky now. Do you think you could make me a cup of tea, Becky? You ought to be able to manage that, at least!"

"I ... I'm really sorry," said Becky. As she gathered together the mugs and took them away to wash up, her eyes blurred with tears. Perhaps this is all I'm fit for, she thought, sniffing forlornly. I should have realized that message was urgent, should have noticed that Sandie hadn't come in...

If only it hadn't been Sandie, she thought ruefully. She doesn't need any excuses to have a go at me!

"What are you looking so fed up about?" said Linda, when Becky brought in the tea.

Becky explained what had happened, feeling very shamefaced. To her surprise, Linda actually laughed.

"Oh, cheer up, it's not the end of the world," she said. "You weren't to know that Sandie was going straight to Kensington today. And you had plenty of other work to do this morning, besides taking Sandie's messages. Don't worry about it, Becky!"

But Becky couldn't help worrying. I want to get everything right, she thought. This job means so much to me, I can't afford to make mistakes. Especially with people like Sandie around!

She was still mulling it all over when she got back to Croydon that evening. Kate took one look at her miserable face and smiled sympathetically.

"Don't tell me," she said. "You had a bad day at work!"

"Uh? Sorry, what was that?" said Becky, who had been imagining Linda and the Editor calling her into the office and telling her, ever so regretfully, that they were sorry but they didn't think she was cut out to be a journalist, after all. What would I do? she thought. I couldn't go home, I just couldn't! What would everyone say? Mum and Dad? Jan? Nick...?

Suddenly she realized that Kate was speaking to her.

"Becky? What is it? You haven't been listening to a word I said!"

Becky sighed. "Sorry, Kate. It's just that I made an awful mistake today..."

"What did you do?"

Becky explained, and Kate sniffed. "Goodness, is that all? From the look on your face, I thought the whole magazine must have been destroyed, at the very least! Listen, if that's the worst mistake you ever make at work, you'll be doing better than most of us, I can tell you. I made a couple of really awful blunders when I started."

"Did you?" said Becky, faintly cheered by Kate's attitude. All the same, she thought, this is the time when I could do with a letter or a phone call from Nick. He used to be great when I had problems, like when I had that row with Suzanne Chalmers. He was the one who calmed us both down. But now, I ... I'm not sure he even cares any more...

Why does life have to be so complicated? What with Nick's moods, and Sandie Johnson taking a dislike to me...

When she told Kate about the flat, she simply nodded thoughtfully.

"Its up to you, Becky," she said. "I don't want you to feel you have to find your own place straight away. You're no trouble to Graham and me, you know that. We shall miss you; we've loved having you with us, haven't we, Charlie Boy? But if this flat turns out to be OK, I think it'd be good for you. Give you a chance to meet some new people, take your mind off Nick!"

Becky was startled. I'm not sure that I *want* anything taking my mind off Nick, she thought. Kate obviously thinks I should forget him, find someone else. But it's just not that easy.

"It's been great living here," she said sincerely, "but I do want to try living in a flat, you know? Anyway, I haven't seen it yet; it might be awful, or the other girls might decide they don't want me. Fi asked me round to supper tomorrow night; is that all right?"

"Fine," said Kate. "We'll expect you when we see you, then, shall we? And I wouldn't worry about that Sandie girl, either. She sounds like a pain in the neck, if you ask me. There's one in every office."

In spite of everything her aunt had said, Becky found it hard to settle down and relax that evening. *If I was at home,* she thought, flicking through the latest issue of the magazine without taking any of it in, *I'd go round to Nick's right now and have a moan to him. Or Jan...*

But she had only just written to Nick and Jan. She didn't want to use the office phone to call him, because everyone, including Sandie Johnson, would hear her. Nor did she like to keep asking Kate if she could use the phone to make long-distance calls. Her parents had always been strict about that.

"When you pay the bills, you can rabbit on for as long as you like," she remembered her dad telling her in exasperation. "For heaven's sake, Becky, you and Jan are together all day at school. What do you find to talk about for half the evening as well?"

In the end, he'd limited her phone calls to ten minutes.

"That way, your mum and I might get the chance to use it too!" he told her with a grin.

In the end, it was Kate who suggested that Becky phoned Nick.

"Would you mind?" Becky said.

"No, of course not. Off you go!"

Becky jumped up and headed for the phone in the hall.

She heard the ringing tone, far away, and then a woman's voice saying "Hello?"

"Oh, Mrs Miller, it's Becky!"

"Becky! Hello, dear, how are you? How's the job going?"

"Fine," said Becky, conscious of the minutes ticking away. "Mrs Miller, is Nick there?"

"No, I'm afraid he's not," his mother said. "He's gone out with some of the other lads. I'm not sure when he'll be back; it might be quite late..."

Becky felt sick with disappointment.

"I'll tell him you called, shall I?" Mrs Miller went on.

Becky nodded, and then, realizing that Nick's mum couldn't see her, managed to say, "Yes, please."

"Nice to hear from you anyway, Becky. Pop in when you come home, won't you? We want to hear all about your exciting life in London, you know!"

Exciting life in London, Becky thought miserably. If they only knew. Fi had asked her to go out clubbing a couple of times, but she was worried about missing Nick, if he called. Not that he called that often.

"Well?" Kate demanded when she went back into the living-room.

"He wasn't there. He'd gone out," said Becky.

"Never mind, love. Tomorrow is another day, as they say," said Kate sympathetically.

"Let's hope it's better than this one," Becky groaned. Charlie Boy jumped on to her lap and settled down, purring like a lawnmower. It's all right for cats, Becky thought. They never have to worry about bad-tempered colleagues, or boyfriends who aren't around when you need them!

For almost the first time since she'd started the job, Becky's heart sank when she woke up in the morning and thought about going to work. I wonder what sort of mood Sandie will be in today, she thought apprehensively.

But she need not have worried. As soon as she arrived, Paula told her that Sandie had gone to do her re-scheduled interview with Apocalypse, and wouldn't be in until the afternoon. It felt like a weight lifting from Becky's shoulders and she began to plough through a pile of short-story manuscripts with a light heart.

"OK for tonight, Becky?" Fi said, sticking her red head around the door. "You're taking your life in your hands, I hope you realize!"

"What on earth do you mean?"

"Sampling my special spaghetti Bolognese. It's not so much Bolognese, more sort of Camberwell, really!"

Becky burst out laughing.

The two girls caught a bus right outside the office and even in the rush hour, it was barely fifteen minutes before they had to get off. Fi led the way along the main road, down a side street, and then another, and stopped in front of a large shabby Edwardian house. The front garden was paved over and a few straggly shrubs grew in the flower-bed.

"Here we are," Fi said. "It's no palace, but it's home! We're upstairs. A couple of nurses live on the ground floor. They're very nice, but we hardly ever see them."

She led the way up a worn staircase and opened another door, which led on to a narrow landing. The living-room was at the front of the house and was cluttered with a huge, sagging sofa, no less than three armchairs, and several pieces of dark, old-fashioned furniture. Two girls were curled up on the sofa watching TV, but they got up and switched off when Fi and Becky came in.

"This is Becky," said Fi. "Becky, these are my flatmates, Ruth Brown and Jade Pennington."

"Hello," said Becky, feeling suddenly shy, even though both girls were smiling at her in a friendly way. Jade was very pretty and slim, with long, straight blonde hair. Ruth seemed rather older, in her early 20s, Becky guessed, with curly dark hair and glasses.

"Make yourself at home, Becky," Ruth said. "This is the living-room, as you can see, and there are two decent-sized bedrooms."

"That means you'll be sharing with me," Fi put in. "I hope you don't snore, Becky!"

"I … I don't think so!" Becky said.

"Tell you what," Fi went on, "why don't you two show Becky round, while I put the spaghetti on?"

"OK," said Jade, speaking for the first time, in a soft Welsh accent. "Come this way, Becky!"

They showed her the room she'd be sharing with Fi, their own bedroom, and the bathroom, which contained the biggest, oldest bath Becky had ever seen!

"A real museum-piece, isn't it?" Jade giggled. "There's hardly ever enough hot water for more than about six inches, and it's freezing cold in winter!"

The kitchen wasn't exactly state-of-the-art either, with an old-fashioned gas stove and an ancient enamel sink. Fi, wrapped in a striped butcher's apron, was stirring strands and strands of spaghetti into boiling water.

"Well?" she said. "Do you think you can bear the idea of living here?"

Becky blushed. "If ... if you can bear to have me!" she said.

Fi looked at Jade, and at Ruth, who had come up behind the other two and was standing in the kitchen doorway. They were all smiling.

"Welcome home, Becky!" Fi said.

5

"I think that's the lot!" Becky gasped, as she dragged another black plastic bag of clothes along the landing and into the bedroom.

"I hope you're going to be able to fit everything in," said Ruth doubtfully, looking around the room, already more than half-full with Fi's belongings.

"Oh, don't worry," Fi said cheerfully. "I don't think Becky's got half as many clothes as Lorraine had. Come to that, Jade's a fashion fanatic too. Well, she would be, wouldn't she, being a model? We'll soon find space for Becky's things, no problem."

Ruth disappeared to make coffee.

"This is going to work out really well, I know it is," said Becky. "I'm going to be spending so much less on transport, and I won't have to get up so early."

She and Fi went into the living-room, where Nick sat awkwardly in an armchair and Jade on the sofa. As they went in, Becky heard Jade's soft Welsh voice say, "What is it you do, then, Nick?"

"Not a lot," said Nick, and relapsed into silence.

Oh, no, Becky thought. He might at least try to make conversation! He'd been like that in Croydon, where Kate and Graham had done their best to draw him out, get him to talk about himself. He'd been abrupt to the point of rudeness, answering all their friendly questions in monosyllables and making it obvious he couldn't wait to leave.

All the way to Camberwell in the van – they'd got lost twice, and it was Becky's fault both times – she'd wondered whether she ought to say something, but in the end she didn't. After all, Nick had come all the way to London to help her move. He'll loosen up, once he gets to know the girls a bit, she thought hopefully. Ruth and Fi were both outgoing, chatty types. Jade was quieter, though she'd obviously been doing her best to talk to Nick. He might make an effort, Becky thought in exasperation.

When Ruth brought the coffee in, Jade looked positively relieved. She drank hers quickly and then went to her room, murmuring something about getting changed to meet her boyfriend.

"Jade's a fashion model," said Ruth proudly, "and her boyfriend's a photographer, Ben Grainger. You might have heard of him."

"No," said Nick.

Oh dear, Becky thought. "Ruth's a medical secretary," she said hastily. That sounds a bit more ... well, ordinary. Not so glamorous, she thought.

"So what are you two planning to do this week-end?" asked Fi pleasantly. "Some of Ruth's friends from the hospital and I are going out for a Chinese tonight, then on to a club. You're welcome to join us…"

Becky thought that sounded fun, but Nick frowned.

"Don't be silly, Fi," Ruth said. "Nick and Becky haven't seen each other for ages. I bet he's planning a romantic dinner for two, aren't you?"

"Er … well, something like that," said Nick, looking embarrassed.

"*Chez Pierre* in the High Street isn't bad," said Fi, "and it's a whole lot cheaper than the West End!"

"I'm not so hard up I can't afford to take Becky out for a decent meal!" Nick snapped. "We'll go wherever you want, Becky! The West End, if you like!"

There was an embarrassed silence.

"I'm sorry," said Fi. "I didn't mean…"

"Of course you didn't," said Becky, shocked. How *could* Nick be so touchy? He should have realized that Fi was only trying to help, since neither of them knew the area.

"Sorry," Nick growled.

Ruth drained her coffee mug and stood up. "Come on, Fi," she said. "I want to go up to Oxford Street to look for some shoes to go with that blue dress I bought last week."

Becky felt like bursting into tears. She wanted Nick to get on with her new flatmates. After all, they could easily object to him coming to stay for weekends. The flat wasn't that big. So why did he have to start by showing them the worst, the very worst, side of himself?

"Oh, Nick," she began helplessly, "did you have to?"

"I hate being patronized," Nick said sulkily.

"But Fi didn't mean it like that, you idiot!"

"Oh, maybe she didn't. But there was that other girl, that model, asking me about myself, pretending to be interested..."

"But she *was* interested!" cried Becky, exasperated. "I've told them all about you, of course I have!"

"Don't be daft. Why would some snotty fashion model be interested in a guy like me?"

"Oh, I give up," snapped Becky. "Jade isn't the least snotty. She's a very sweet, down-to-earth girl from the Rhondda valley, who just happens to work as a model, and she's interested in talking to you because you're my boyfriend."

Nick just grunted bad-temperedly and Becky went to her room to sort out her belongings. I'm beginning to wish I'd never asked him to come down here, she thought.

By the time she had squeezed her clothes into her half of the wardrobe and arranged her CD collection in the living-room, the flat had already begun to look more like home and Nick was in a better temper. She'd sent him out to buy a pint of milk. He came back with a big bunch of chrysanthemums and gave her a kiss.

"Sorry, Becky. I got these for you," he said, rather shamefacedly.

After that, things seemed to get better. Nick and Becky took a bus as far as the river and walked along beside it, Becky pointing out all the landmarks, including her own office!

"How are things at home, really?" she asked him. "Have you thought any more about doing resits or anything?"

Nick shrugged. "Doesn't seem much point," he said, "since I don't really know what I want to do. And I can't face the idea of any more school."

"Have you been applying for jobs, then?"

"A few."

"No luck so far?"

"No."

Well, you couldn't make a conversation out of that, Becky thought.

In the end, they went to the local French restaurant that Fi had recommended, and it was brilliant. They held hands, rather desperately, across the candlelit table, as if they were never going to meet again. Why can't it always be like this? Becky thought.

Sunday was pouring wet. Nick volunteered to go out and get the papers, and then they all had a good-natured game of Trivial Pursuit. Nick was more like the friendly guy he'd always been, no one said anything tactless, and when he left in the afternoon, Ruth said, "Oh, come down and see us any time, Nick!" as if she really meant it.

Becky watched the tail-lights of his van disappear up the road with a lump in her throat and an ache in her heart. It could've been worse, she thought. It could've been a whole lot worse...

At least she had work to take her mind off her love-life, she thought in the office next morning. Her spirits lifted even more when Paula reminded her that Sandie wouldn't be in that week. She'd gone off to Turkey on a late-summer break. Good, Becky thought. At least I won't have her breathing down my neck and looking for excuses to have a go at me!

Linda came in, waving an envelope. "Anyone heard of a band called 'Rags'?" she enquired.

Paula thought for a moment then shook her head. Becky frowned.

"I might have," she said. "I think they were on that Channel Four pop show last week."

"Any good?"

"Yes, they weren't bad. Sort of pop-rock, with a very good-looking lead singer," said Becky. "Why?"

"I've been invited to their launch party and showcase gig on Friday," said Linda. "It's at the 49 Club in Soho. I can't go, though. Would you like the invitation, Becky?"

"Me?" said Becky, taken aback. She was so used to Sandie snapping up all the invitations to gigs, launch parties, and record-company bashes that she had almost given up the idea of going to anything like that herself.

"Yes, you!" laughed Linda. "I know Sandie normally does this kind of thing but she's not here, is she? Anyway, it's time you had a go at something like that."

"All right," said Becky, trying to look as though lunch dates with pop groups came her way every day. Good job Sandie isn't here, she thought. She'd be sure to come out with some sarky remark, or grab the invitation for herself, more likely!

Becky arrived at the 49 Club at lunchtime on Friday, feeling rather nervous. She handed her invitation to a snooty-looking doorman. Inside, at a small table, sat an orange-haired girl a little older than herself, checking off names on a list.

"I'm Becky Rivers," said Becky. Her voice came out as a sort of croak and she had to clear her throat. "I'm here instead of Linda Hobson ... I telephoned..."

"Oh, yes," said the orange-haired girl with a bright smile. "I'm Stella, Press Officer for BK Records. Hi, Becky. You can leave your coat, then go downstairs to the bar and help yourself to a drink and something to eat. The band will be doing a four-song spot in about half an hour. Don't forget to pick up a press kit on your way out!"

Becky followed a crowd of other people down the stairs and into a cramped, dark bar area. It was so crowded she could hardly move and there seemed no chance of getting to the bar. Not that she wanted a drink, anyway.

For a panic-stricken moment, she was tempted to turn and flee. What was she, Becky Rivers, doing here anyway? In a room full of glamorous strangers, all talking at the tops of their voices and seeming to know one another? As she watched, two girls in impossibly tight leather trousers squealed "Darling!" at one another and gave each other air-kisses on both cheeks. I'll never fit in, Becky thought despairingly, it's no use...

"You look lost!" said a cheerful male voice beside her.

Becky swung round with a gasp and found herself looking into a pair of twinkling, hazel-green eyes. The guy who had spoken looked young, no more than twenty, with thick dusty-blond hair and a friendly grin.

"It's like a battle-zone, isn't it?" he said sympathetically. "I suppose I ought to be glad we've pulled in such a good crowd, but it's hopeless if you want a drink or anything to eat!"

He said "we", Becky thought shyly; that means he must be something to do with the band. Or maybe...

"Are you from BK Records?" she shouted, trying to make herself heard above the music and the conversation.

"Me? No, I work for Russ Proctor, Rags' manager," the guy said. "My name's Shaun Carswell, what's yours?"

"Becky Rivers. I'm from *Ace* magazine!"

"Oho!" said Shaun. "A journalist, eh? One of these powerful people who can make or break a band, so we're told! I shall have to be very, very nice to you, young woman!"

Becky giggled, liking him at once. The idea of her being a powerful, influential journalist was too funny for words! She felt more like a little kid on her first day a school.

"Let me start by getting you a drink," said Shaun. "I bet my elbows are stronger than yours!

What would you like?"

"Orange juice, please," said Becky firmly.

By some miracle, Shaun managed to force his way to the bar and come back with a beer for himself and a delicious glass of freshly-squeezed orange juice for Becky. He smiled at her.

"So *Ace* magazine is interested in Rags, is it?" he said.

"Sort of," Becky admitted. "The Features Editor sent me along today and said if they were good we might put them on our pop page. We have a New Talent spot, they could go in there."

"Have you heard them before?"

"I think so," said Becky. "They were on TV last week, weren't they?"

Shaun nodded. "Glad you noticed," he said. "They're a good little band, Becky, though I say it myself. They're from Scotland, been together since schooldays, write their own songs, nothing hyped or artificial about them. They were doing gigs up in Glasgow and put out a couple of indie singles on their own label before one of the BK scouts recommended them to us."

Becky nodded, wondering what a scout was. A talent scout, she supposed. Shaun looked at his watch.

"They'll be on in a minute," he said. "Would you like to go to the front, Becky, nearer the stage? They're worth seeing, honestly."

He put his hand under her elbow to steer her towards the tiny stage at the far end of the room. Suddenly, Becky felt self-conscious. Shaun seemed to be making a big fuss of her, an insignificant,

74

junior journalist on a teenage magazine. There must be more important people he could be talking to, she thought uneasily. Why me?

But she had no time to say anything because crashing power-chords announced Rags' first number. There was a skinny boy in a white T-shirt on guitar, a bass-player with curly dark hair, a girl keyboardist and a powerful drummer who looked a bit older than the others.

The good-looking singer she'd noticed on TV was the real star, though. Without a sign of nerves, he led the band through two out-and-out rockers, a tender ballad, and then another powerful rocker. By the time the band had reached the end of the last song, Becky was a firm fan. Shaun was right, she thought, exhilarated. They are special!

"Thanks for coming to see us," drawled the singer confidently. "We're doing a club tour next month and we hope to see you there!"

There was a burst of applause as the band disappeared backstage. Shaun turned to Becky, his eyes alight with enthusiasm.

"Well?" he demanded. "What did you think?"

"I loved it!" said Becky truthfully. "Great songs, great image. I'm sure they'll make it!"

"Really?" said Shaun, looked pleased. As his hazel eyes met hers, Becky looked away in confusion. He really seems to care what I think, she thought. Why? I'm nobody special!

"I thought they were brillant," she insisted.

"Would you like to see them again?"

"I'd love to."

"Well, you heard what Paul said, they'll be

touring in November. If you give me your number, I'll call you when the dates are announced."

He's just being professional, Becky thought. It's nothing personal. Shaun's not chatting me up, or anything like that. He couldn't be...

Then she looked up, caught Shaun's eye, and felt a strange fluttery sensation in the pit of her stomach, as though she was going down too fast in a lift.

"Your number, Becky?" he reminded her gently.

"Oh, yes," she said, taking her notebook out of her bag and scribbling down the office number. Shaun tucked the folded piece of paper into his wallet.

"Now, how about something to eat, Becky?" he asked. "You can't do a hard day's ... well, afternoon's work on an empty stomach!"

Becky was about to reply that she wasn't very hungry and that anyway, she really ought to be getting back to the office, but Shaun didn't give her a chance. Instead, he steered her over to the other side of the room where a delicious-looking buffet was spread out and people were already loading their plates. He even managed to find a relatively quiet corner, next to the stage, where they could rest their plates and glasses on a window-sill.

"How long have you worked on the magazine?" he asked her, munching.

"Not quite two months," said Becky, nibbling at a tiny, spicy vol-au-vent. "Mmm, this is delicious!"

"What did you do before?"

"I was at school!" Becky admitted. "I always

wanted to be a journalist, though, so when my exams were over I wrote to Linda, the Features Editor, and she gave me a summer job. Then, when she told me there was a permanent job going, I jumped at it!"

"Good for you!" said Shaun admiringly. "I guess journalism is like the music business in a way. Jobs are hardly ever advertised. If you want one, you really have to hustle for it!"

"Is that what you did?" Becky asked.

Shaun nodded. "I started off as a studio tape op," he said. Then, as Becky looked blank, he explained. "It's the dogsbody job in a recording studio, cleaning up all the beer-cans and running round after the engineers who actually use the equipment. Then I got to know Russ through the studio boss, and he persuaded me to move over to management. Russ is brilliant, one of the best managers in the business. I've learned such a lot from him."

"I know," said Becky. "I know heaps more about magazines then I did before, just from listening to Linda and Paula at work…"

"So you're aiming to be a top journalist one day, are you?"

Becky hesitated for a moment, then nodded. Suddenly, being ambitious, wanting to get right to the top, do as well as she possibly could in her chosen career, seemed OK again.

"Yes," she said firmly. "Yes, that's what I want!"

"Me too," Shaun agreed. "I mean, I want to have my own management company one day."

Becky looked around her and realized that the

crowded club was now half-empty! She glanced at her watch and saw that it was half-past two.

"Shaun, I've got to go," she said, draining her glass of orange juice. "And I've just remembered, Linda asked me if I could get a quote from the band."

Shaun shook his head. "Not this time," he said. "I know Russ doesn't want them doing any interviews until just before the album comes out. I'll tell Stella, their press girl, and she'll make sure you get priority!"

Together, Becky and Shaun strolled over to the exit, where the orange-haired girl was sitting beside a pile of cardboard folders.

"Hi, Becky," she said. "Glad you could come. What did you think of the band?"

"I thought they were very good," said Becky. "Especially the singer!"

"He's a real star, Paul, isn't he?" Stella agreed. "Here's your press kit, Becky, with a copy of the CD. It'll be out next month."

"I've got to go, Becky," said Shaun, touching her lightly on the shoulder. "Nice meeting you. I'll be in touch about the gig, OK?"

Again, as Shaun's eyes me hers, Becky had that strange hollow sensation in her stomach. What's the matter with me? she thought. Anyone would think I'd never met a good-looking guy before...

Aha, so you *do* think Shaun Carswell is attractive, said the voice of her conscience. Admit it, Becky. That is one seriously fanciable guy ... and he's been talking to you for what? An hour and a half? And he took your telephone number. You've been chatted up, Becky Rivers, no two ways about that!

She was feeling very thoughtful as she made her way back to the Tube station and the office. On her way, she read the biography of Rags that was in her press kit. "The band are managed by Russ Proctor, who has worked with some of the biggest names in the business," she read. Shaun's name, of course, wasn't mentioned. But every time Becky thought of a certain pair of twinkling hazel eyes, a friendly smile, and a shock of dark-blond hair, a shiver ran down her spine. *I wonder if he will phone about that gig. I wonder if he'll remember,* she caught herself thinking. When the Tube train stopped at Waterloo, she was so deeply lost in a daydream that she almost forgot to get off!

"Well?" Paula demanded when she got back to the office. "How did it go?"

"OK," said Becky vaguely, trying to push the mental image of Shaun Carswell right to the back of her mind. *I'll probably never see him again, anyway,* she told herself firmly.

"What were the band like?" Paula asked.

"I thought they were really good," Becky said. "I didn't speak to them, but I did ... er ... meet someone from their management who said they'd be doing interviews when their album comes out, and gigs too."

Paula was flipping through the press kit that Becky had left on the desk. "Ooh, that one's nice! He'd make a great pin-up!" she said.

Becky glanced over her shoulder and laughed. "That's Paul, the singer. Tasty, isn't he?"

"Not half!"

Becky looked at Paul's brooding face and sexy, rock-star pout and sighed. He was very attractive, but not her type at all. She liked casual, friendly guys, who weren't posers. Guys like Nick...

Or Shaun Carswell...

Linda came in while she and Paula were still looking at the photos. She bent over them too.

"We could certainly use that guy as a pin-up!" she said. "Or maybe Lisa could use him in a fashion spread."

"I was told that they weren't doing any interviews until the album comes out next month," Becky said, her heart thumping. If Linda wanted Paul and Rags to appear in the magazine, she'd have a good chance of seeing Shaun again!

Linda said that that was OK, but then Becky thought of something else. With a sinking heart, she remembered Sandie Johnson. She wouldn't be too pleased to come back from her holiday in Turkey to find Becky arranging an interview with a pop group! She'd already made it clear that the pop side of the magazine was her department, and Becky didn't want to tread on her toes, or get on the wrong side of her again!

"Er," she began, feeling awkward, "will Sandie be doing the interview? When she comes back, I mean?"

Linda looked surprised. "Why should she?" she said. "I'm sure Sandie has enough on her plate already!"

"But she usually does the pop interviews..." said Becky.

"Only because I don't want to," put in Paula. "I'm tone-deaf anyway, and can hardly tell Phil Collins from George Michael!"

"No, no," said Linda, "you try this one, Becky. You've seen the band, and liked them. It's about time you did an interview for us. You've got to start some day!"

Becky nodded. With half her mind, she was thrilled at being given the chance to do some proper writing – and an interview with a real-life pop singer, at that! With the other half, she felt scared to death. Quite apart from worrying about what she would say to the good-looking stranger in the photos, she couldn't help worrying about Sandie.

She rang Stella, Rags' press officer, to put in her request for an interview and possibly a fashion session with Paul. Stella sounded so friendly and helpful that Becky felt better at once.

"I'll ring you as soon as I know when they're coming in," Stella promised. "And I'll call Russ, their manager, and find out how he feels about Paul doing a fashion spread as well."

At the sound of Russ Proctor's name, Becky felt her hands go clammy. That's Shaun's boss, she thought. He might even take the call. Not that it matters to me, of course...

She was so busy that afternoon that she was able, with a determined effort, to push the thought of Shaun Carswell right to the back of her mind. It was her turn to cook dinner, so on her way home she concentrated on the menu she'd planned.

Fi had already told her she was working late, so Jade was the only one of her flatmates who was in when she got home.

"Hi," she said. "Had a good day?"

Jade made a face. "Not specially," she said. "I went to a casting for a soft-drink commercial, but I didn't get it. The girl they picked was awful, thighs like an elephant and a huge bum to match!"

Becky grinned to herself. Jade had a typical model's figure – five foot eight and a perfect size 10. According to her, anyone any bigger was fat!

"I'm sorry," she said gently. "Better luck next time, eh?"

"S'pose so," Jade shrugged. "Oh, by the way, there was a letter for you, Becky!"

"For me? It's probably my friend from home, Jan."

But as Jade handed her the envelope and she recognized the writing, she felt a guilty pang. It wasn't from Jan...

It was from Nick.

6

Becky turned Nick's letter over and over in her hands. He'd called her to let her know he'd got home safely, but this was the first letter she'd had from him for a while. Jade was looking at her curiously.

"Well?" she demanded. "Aren't you going to open it?"

"Um," said Becky helplessly. "I … I don't think it's from Jan after all. It's from Nick!"

"Oh," said Jade.

Becky didn't know whether to laugh or cry. She still wasn't sure what the girls thought of Nick. He certainly hadn't done much to endear himself to them on Saturday, though Sunday had gone more smoothly.

"Have you and Nick been together long?" Jade had asked her, after Nick left. Becky explained the problem: their year-long relationship, Nick's failed exams and ruined plans.

"I thought he seemed a bit … well … moody,"

was Jade's only comment. Fi, typically, was more outspoken.

"If it's meant to last, it will do," she had consoled Becky. "Sounds to me like he's still fed up about failing his exams. Blokes are like that, you know. A girl would've had a good cry, moaned to her mates, and then picked herself up and started making plans. That's what I'd do, anyway."

"Me, too," said Becky thoughtfully.

"Meanwhile," said Fi with a grin, "London's full of guys, Becky! It's a shame to stay in, waiting by the phone, when you could be out having fun!"

But Becky didn't want to think about that. And, most especially, she didn't want to think about Shaun Carswell. Not here. Not now, with a letter from Nick in her hand...

"'Scuse me, Jade. I just want to see what he says," she said as she fled to the privacy of her bedroom.

"OK. I'll make you a cup of tea, shall I? The kettle's just boiled," her flatmate replied.

Becky read her letter with a growing sense of guilt. It was almost as though Nick *knew*, in some mysterious telepathic way, that she'd just met another attractive guy. She had been disappointed in Nick's letters so far. Not that she expected romance. She knew Nick too well for that. But ... strings of excuses for why he hadn't written before, plus descriptions of the football matches he'd played in, weren't what she been hoping for.

But this time, he asked her when she was coming home for the weekend, told her how much he was missing her and how wonderful it had been to see her. There were four kisses under the scrawl that was his name. It was the sort of letter she'd been hoping for, longing for...

So why didn't she feel happier about it? He loved her, he was missing her, wasn't that what she wanted?

She folded his letter up and put it in her writing-case. Maybe I *should* go home for a weekend and see him, she thought guiltily. I did say I would...

But there was always so much to do, what with the new job, and moving from Kate and Graham's, and settling into the flat. I can't go next weekend, it's Fi's birthday, Becky thought, and the weekend after that Ruth's got us all tickets for the ballet. It's not that I don't want to go home. I know Mum and Dad would love to see me, and there's Emily, and Jan, too, as well as Nick.

She was looking very thoughtful as she went back into the living-room.

"Everything OK?" said Jade, handing her a mug of tea.

"I suppose so," sighed Becky. "Nick wants to know when I can go home for a weekend. I did promise I would, but it won't be for a couple of weeks."

Just then, Fi came in with the shopping. "What are you two skivers doing in here?" she demanded. "I thought it was Becky's turn to make dinner?"

"Oh, no! I forgot to put the casserole in!" wailed Becky, setting down her mug and heading for the kitchen at a run. Fi and Jade both giggled. When she came back into the living-room, Fi said, "Jade tells me you've heard from Nick, Becky!"

"That's right. He wants me to go home for a weekend."

"Good idea," Fi said. "Sounds like you need to have a chat with him. I mean, either you and Nick are together or you're not. You haven't been out with anyone else since you've been down here..."

She broke off as she noticed Becky's scarlet cheeks.

"Becky? You haven't, have you? You *are* a dark horse, not saying anything! Who is he? What's he like? Where did you meet him?"

"It's nothing," said Becky, feeling horribly embarrassed. How could she tell the girls about Shaun? And what was there to tell, anyway? She would probably never see him again.

"Nothing? Then why are you blushing like that?" teased Jade.

"Well," said Becky, "isn't it awful, the way everything happens at once?"

"It does with guys," said Jade. "They're like London buses. You don't see one for ages, then two or three come along at the same time!"

Becky couldn't help laughing.

"You know that press reception I went to at lunchtime, for a new band called Rags? I met a really nice guy there. He works for the band's manager. We talked for ages and he took my number and said he'd call me when the band were playing in London."

"Sounds OK to me," said Fi. "What did he look like?"

"Oh … nice," said Becky. "Not flashy or anything, he just had on jeans and a T-shirt. Darkish blond hair, sort of greeny eyes, not especially tall, really friendly. I don't know, though. I'm probably making something out of nothing. His boss probably told him it was Be Nice to Journalists Day or something!"

"Did he chat up anyone else?" asked Jade.

"No, he spent most of the time with me."

"There you are, then. Sounds like he's keen. Did you give him this number, or the office one?"

"The office one. I thought that sounded more professional. I … I wasn't really sure whether he was chatting me up or not, you see," Becky explained, feeling very young and rather silly. Nothing is ever going to be simple and straightforward any more, she thought with a sudden flash of insight. And no one except me can decide what to do. It's my choice, my decision.

"I bet he calls you!" grinned Jade.

Becky wasn't sure whether she hoped Jade was right, or not.

"Where's the harm in a casual date?" said Fi. "He can't eat you. And it's no fun sitting in every night watching TV."

"But what about Nick?"

"Fix up to go and see him for a weekend, and sort things out then," Fi advised. "You won't know how you feel till you've seen him again, and in the meantime…"

"What?"

"Is there any chance we might get something to eat tonight, before we die of starvation? I'm sure I can hear Ruth coming in!"

Becky flung a cushion at her friend and disappeared into the kitchen. Fi's right, she thought, as she chopped vegetables, one eye on her cookery book propped up in a corner. I will have to go home for a weekend soon. And if Shaun rings, well, a casual date can't do any harm.

For the rest of that week at work, Becky's heart leapt into her throat every time the telephone rang. It seemed to ring more often than usual and she always seemed to be the one to answer it, her palms damp with sweat and her mouth dry. When she heard a male voice at the other end, her "Features Department?" came out like a kind of croak.

But it was never Shaun.

She wrote to Nick, a long, gossipy letter telling him about all the things she'd been doing, including going to her very first press reception and seeing a band called Rags. Nick loved music. He'd even got a band together when they were in the fourth year, but it hadn't lasted long.

"I'll come home for a weekend soon, I promise," she finished up. "It seems ages and ages since I left. I do get homesick sometimes, you know."

She paused, tempted to cross out that last line. Did she get homesick? Her life was so different now, so full, so busy, that it was hard to find time even to think how she felt. She'd felt a bit weepy those first few nights at Kate's but since she'd moved into the flat there'd been so much going on. She was glad to get letters and phone calls from her mum and dad and Jan, and to be kept in touch with all the gossip from home. It seemed like another world...

She still loved her job and Linda seemed pleased with her. Becky suspected she'd had a word with Sandie Johnson, because even she was less catty. She wasn't exactly friendly, but she had stopped jumping down Becky's throat for every little thing.

She wasn't too thrilled when Linda told her that Becky would be doing an interview with Rags for the pop page, though!

"You don't mind, do you?" Linda said breezily. "It's only half a page for the New Talent spot, and as Becky has already spoken to the record company about it... Anyway, it'll be good practice for her."

"I didn't know you wanted to go into music journalism, Becky," said Sandie, rather frostily.

"I'm not sure if I do," Becky confessed. "I want to try everything!"

"Well, rather you than me," sniffed Sandie. "New bands are a pain. And that guy Paul looks like he thinks he's God's gift to women."

"I'm sure Becky can cope," said Linda comfortingly. Becky gulped. She wasn't at all sure! Trust Sandie to try and put me off, she thought. But since she spent most of the morning moaning about how much work she had to do, she can hardly complain if Linda gives me one measly interview!

She was just about to pick up the phone to call Rags' press officer when it rang. "Yes? Features

Department?" she said, half her mind on the questions she was planning to ask the singer. Her very first pop interview! It was really exciting.

"Could I speak to Becky Rivers, please?"

"Yes, speaking!"

"Becky, it's Shaun Carswell. Remember me? We met at the BK Records press reception the other week…"

Becky was so startled that she nearly dropped the phone. "Oh … hi, Shaun!" she said weakly.

"Becky, are you still there?"

"Yes, of course I am," said Becky. Work problems, the wet weather, Sandie's bitchiness, suddenly didn't seem to matter any more. Shaun had rung her! He was there, waiting, on the other end of a telephone line. Waiting for her…

"Have you had a copy of Rags' tour dates yet? I asked Stella at BK to make sure she sent them to you."

"I don't think so," said Becky, trying to sound as efficient and professional as she could, even though her pulse was racing and she was sure her blush was lighting up the entire office!

"They're playing the Bottom Line on the eighteenth," Shaun told her. "Do you think you can make it?"

"I'm sure I can," said Becky, hoping she didn't sound too eager. Desperation puts guys off more than anything else, she remembered Jan saying once. It never does any harm to play it cool…

But if I'm too cool, Becky thought, Shaun will think I'm not interested. And am I? Am I interested in Rags the band, or in Shaun Carswell?

"I'll see you there, then," Shaun was saying. "Stella will send you tickets, and a backstage pass, if you want to come round and meet the guys after the gig."

"That would be wonderful!"

"Er…" Shaun went on, "do you need two tickets, Becky?"

"What do you mean?" asked Becky, puzzled.

"Well, will you be bringing anyone? Because I was wondering … maybe you'd like to meet for a drink before the gig?"

"Meet?" Becky almost squeaked. "You mean … meet you?"

She heard Shaun chuckle at the other end of the line. "Yes, of course, meet me! If you think you can stand it, that is!"

Suddenly, Becky stopped feeling shy and self-conscious. What fun he is, she thought. She remembered the easy, friendly chat they'd had the first time they met. There's nothing to worry about, she thought. It'll all work out. I'll be all right with Shaun.

"I'd like that," she said demurely. They arranged when and where to meet and Becky replaced the receiver gently. I've got a date, she thought.

"Blimey! What's happened? You look like the cat that's got the cream! Did you get a pay rise or something?" said Ruth, when Becky arrived home that evening.

"No, but I got something almost as good. My very first pop interview!" said Becky.

Jade gave a gasp. "Does that mean he rang you? Shaun rang you?" she asked.

Becky nodded. "He wants to meet me for a drink before the gig, and take me backstage to meet the band afterwards," she said.

"It's time you started going out and enjoying yourself, instead of staying in every night hoping Nick will call," said Ruth. "If you ask me, it wouldn't do him any harm at all to drop a few hints about Shaun in your next letter. It might make him buck his ideas up a bit. Treat 'em mean, keep 'em keen is my motto."

But Becky didn't want to do that. It's just a casual date, she told herself firmly. Shaun's a nice person, and attractive, too, and the girls are quite right. I can't stay in every night...

It felt good to be getting ready to go out on a date again. Becky sang in the bath and used a large dollop of her very best bath gel and matching talc. She was planning to wear her black capri pants, the ones that fitted like a second skin, and a black and silver cropped top that Jade had lent her.

You'll do, she told herself, as she peered into her bedroom mirror. She might not have Jade's model figure and natural ash-blonde hair, but her own mousy locks were thick and straight and shiny and her skin was clear. Thank goodness I've grown out of getting spots, she thought gratefully.

She pushed open the door leading to the front bar of the club, hoping that Shaun had already arrived. It was five past eight, so she was neither late nor embarrassingly early. She looked around her uncertainly.

"Becky! I'm really glad you could make it!"

He was there, smiling at her. He wore a black Rags T-shirt and Levi 501s and looked just as she remembered him. He brushed her cheek with his lips before asking her if she wanted a drink.

"Orange juice, please," said Becky, flustered by the kiss. Not that it had been a real kiss, not one that counted. But still...

"How have you been? Looking forward to the gig?" Shaun asked her.

"I'm fine. And yes, very much. Stella says they'll be doing interviews next week."

"That's right. We've set aside a couple of days for press and promotion."

"Actually," Becky confessed, "it'll be the first interview I've ever done!"

"You're kidding!" Shaun raised his eyebrows.

"No, honestly," insisted Becky. "I ... I feel a bit nervous about it..."

"Oh, you won't have any problems with Paul," said Shaun confidently. "Just get him going on his music and he can talk the hind leg off a donkey!"

Becky giggled. "My grandma used to say that about me," she said.

"Oh, you'll get on fine, no problem. He's a nice guy; well, they all are," said Shaun. "Anyway, you're coming backstage with me after the gig, aren't you? I'll introduce you to Paul, tell him you'll be interviewing him, then it won't seem so much like meeting a stranger."

"Thanks," said Becky gratefully. He really understands how I feel, she thought.

"When I was a studio tape op, I used to be scared stiff if anyone well-known came into the studio," Shaun told her. "I once tripped and spilled a cup of coffee over a visiting American band!"

"Oh, no!" Becky gasped. "What happened? What did they say?"

"Nothing. They were really nice about it," said Shaun. "You can't be too star-struck, Becky, when you're working with famous people all the time. You just have to try and do a good job."

"That's what Paula says, one of the writers I work with," said Becky. "But Sandie, the other one, says that new bands are a pain..."

"Some of them are," said Shaun. "They can get a bit bratty once they've got a record deal and start thinking they're superstars. But you won't have any problems with Paul and Rags, I promise."

"Oh, well, that's just typical Sandie," Becky sighed. "Anything that she can say to put me down, or make me feel that I can't do my job, she'll say it."

"Charming!" said Shaun. "Who is this girl, anyway?"

Before she knew what was happening, Becky found herself pouring out the whole story into Shaun's sympathetic ear. Sandie's unfriendly silences and catty remarks, the time she hadn't passed on the telephone message, the way she never missed a chance to have a go at her.

"I wouldn't take any notice if I were you," said Shaun indignantly, when she'd finished. "It sounds like she's the one with problems, not you. Your boss is pleased with you, isn't she?"

"Yes, I think so. It was her idea for me to interview Rags," Becky said.

"You're on your way. Today Rags, tomorrow Michael Jackson," teased Shaun, draining his glass and glancing at his watch.

"Shall we go in?" he said. "Rags are due on in ten minutes."

The club wasn't uncomfortably packed, but there was a good turn out for a new band who had just released their first record, Becky thought. There was a real buzz of excitement in the air, and as the lights dimmed Becky felt a tingle of anticipation. Was it the thought of seeing the band again? Was it because this was her first London gig? Or was it because Shaun Carswell was standing beside her, so close that if she moved more than an inch, she would be in his arms?

He glanced down at her. "OK? Can you see all right?" he asked her.

Becky nodded.

There was a sudden explosion of sound, and Rags erupted, there was no other word for it, on to the stage. From that moment onward, Becky had no chance to think about anything except the music that washed over her, making her want to jump up and down, yell her head off, or dance. Rags played feel-good music, the sort that could carry an audience along with them and leave them feeling drained, breathless, and happy. On stage, they looked ten feet tall.

When it was over, Becky looked at Shaun and breathed, "Wow!"

"Brilliant, aren't they?" he said. "They were a bit nervous about tonight; it was their first real London gig."

"Nervous? You could've fooled me," said Becky admiringly. "Paul's a real star!"

She watched the audience as they left. Almost everyone looked flushed and bright-eyed and smiling. Everyone had had a good time. And so had she...

"Thanks, Shaun," she said impulsively. "I really, really enjoyed that!"

"My pleasure," said Shaun. Their eyes met, and held for a long, breathless moment, until Becky looked away, confused. Oh, help, she thought. I'm not sure I can handle this...

"Got your backstage pass OK?" Shaun said.

"What? Oh ... er ... yes, it's here in my bag somewhere," said Becky, scrabbling. As the crowd thinned out, Becky and Shaun waited beside a door marked "Private. No Admittance". Up on the stage, a team of roadies were dismantling the equipment. A handful of people wearing passes like Becky's hung around, obviously waiting. I wonder who they all are, Becky thought. She felt important, like a real journalist, as one or two of the final stragglers leaving the hall gave her envious glances. They're probably wondering who I am too, she thought.

The door opened and a security guard let them in, checking everyone's passes carefully. Shaun put his arm lightly around Becky and steered her through the crowd, along a brightly-lit corridor, and into an impossibly tiny dressing-room that was already so crammed with people that Becky wondered how she and Shaun were going to squeeze in!

"Is it always like this?" she gasped to Shaun,

"Pretty much!" he told her, grinning. "Better make for that corner over there, Becky. I think I can see a few inches of space."

Becky did as she was told, turned round, and found that Shaun had disappeared. She fought back a sudden feeling of panic. What am I doing here? she thought. Everyone else seems to know someone, to be talking, drinking, laughing. Becky spotted the band's girl keyboard player with a tall guy she vaguely recognized from last week's Top of the Pops. And that stunningly beautiful girl in leather had to be the supermodel who was with the same agency as Jade...

Suddenly Shaun was beside her again. "Sorry about that," he said. "Here, I've brought you a drink, and there's Paul over there. I'll introduce you in a minute."

Becky felt she had never been so glad to see a friendly, familiar face in her life. Now that she had someone to talk to as well she didn't feel so left out, and she and Shaun amused themselves by star-spotting. Wait till I tell Jan about this, Becky thought as she caught sight of her friend's favourite pop star in the crowd. I suppose it wouldn't be cool to ask for an autograph...

Shaun steered her across the room to where Paul, Rags' singer, was surrounded by people.

"This is Becky. She's going to interview you in the week, for *Ace* magazine," said Shaun. Paul beamed at Becky. He *is* good-looking, she thought, dazzled.

"Hi, Becky. Which magazine was it? *Ace*? I don't think I know it..."

"We're a magazine for teenage girls," Becky began.

"Teenage girls? My favourite people!" said Paul, with another cheeky grin. He was a real heartbreaker, Becky decided, but she couldn't help liking him.

"What did you think of the gig, Becky?"

"I loved it," said Becky truthfully. "I saw the showcase you did at the 49 Club but this was much better. The audience was really into it, too."

"Aye," said Paul thoughtfully. "They weren't bad, but you should see our home crowd up in Glasgow! They just go crazy! I keep trying to persuade Shaun to come and see us up there..."

"I will, one day," Shaun promised.

Someone tapped Paul on the shoulder and he turned round. Everyone wants to talk to him, Becky thought. As if he could read her mind, Shaun said, "We'll be off then, Paul. Becky'll see you in the week for the interview."

"I'll look forward to that," Paul said.

Becky's head was still buzzing with noise and excitement as the security guard let her and Shaun out into the street.

"Where d'you live, Becky?" asked Shaun.

"Camberwell. I share a flat."

"That's not far from me; I'm in Lewisham. We could share a cab," said Shaun, hailing a black cab as it drove by. They chatted in a friendly way all the way back until the cab pulled up outside Becky's house.

"Thanks for a lovely evening, Shaun," she said, her hand on the door handle.

"My pleasure," Shaun repeated. "We must do it again some time."

He looked questioningly at her and she could feel her heart thumping. Oh, yes, she thought, I do want to see him again, I really do...

"That would be lovely," she said. "Please call me!"

"I will," said Shaun.

There was a tiny, awkward pause. Is he going to kiss me? Becky thought. Is he? But Shaun made no move, and she didn't know whether to feel relieved or disappointed!

The flat was in darkness when she went in. Beside the phone was a note, addressed to BECKY in large, sprawling capitals. What's this? she thought, half her mind still with Shaun, speeding through the London night to Lewisham. Not far away, he'd said. It would be easy for them to meet again. If he wanted to, and she was pretty sure that he did...

She opened up the note. There were just two words scrawled on the message pad by one of her flatmates.

"Nick phoned!"

7

Becky climbed aboard the Inter-City train at Euston, stowed her overnight bag under her seat and settled down with a Diet Coke and the latest issue of the magazine. It fell open at the pop page and Becky glanced through it. "Interview by Sandie Johnson" it said at the bottom. She felt a twinge of excitement. In just a few weeks her interview with Paul from Rags would be appearing. Underneath, it would say "Interview by Becky Rivers". My very first credit, she thought proudly. I'll keep it for ever and ever!

The interview with Paul had gone very well in spite of Becky's nerves. A cup of tea with Stella, the friendly press officer, helped to calm her down, and when she was finally shown into the interview room and Paul jumped up saying "Hi there. Don't I know you from somewhere?" she actually managed to smile at him.

"I ... I came backstage after your gig. With Shaun Carswell," she told him shyly.

"Becky's with *Ace* magazine," Stella added.

"Oh, yes, the one for teenage girls. Sounds good to me!" grinned Paul. "Well, sit down, sweetheart, make yourself at home!"

When the door closed behind Stella, Becky felt a surge of panic. She took out her little tape-recorder and set it up on the desk next to Paul, hoping he wouldn't notice how much her hands were shaking.

"Tell me about being discovered," she said. "Did you always want to be in a band?"

...Shaun was right, she thought gratefully, twenty minutes later. Paul was a brilliant talker! She had only had to ask him about three questions and he was so relaxed, so friendly, that it was more like chatting to a mate than interviewing a pop star. Eventually, Stella put her head round the door to let Becky know that the next journalist was waiting.

"Is that it?" said Paul. "Have you got everything you want?"

"Yes, I think so," said Becky, feeling weak with relief. Her first interview was over. And she'd managed to get through it without making an idiot of herself.

Paul flashed her one of his devastating smiles. "You'll have to get Shaun to bring you to our next gig," he said.

I wish, Becky thought, but all she said was, "I'd like that!"

I feel like a real journalist, she thought, on her way back to the office. Writing captions and editing the readers' letters is all very well, but interviewing is proper work!

It all helped to take her mind off Shaun. And Nick. And Shaun. And Nick. The two names were spinning round and round in her head until she could hardly think straight. Coming home from her date with Shaun and discovering that Nick had rung her had thrown her completely. What must he have thought, when Ruth told him she was out at a gig and not expected back till late? Would he suspect that she was with someone else?

"Becky, you're being ridiculous," Ruth had told her the next morning. "Why shouldn't you go out to a gig? Nick doesn't expect you to stay in every night, just waiting for him to call, does he?"

"And he doesn't call you often, does he?" Fi had sniffed. "Becky, you must have your own life!"

Becky bit her lip. She could see the girls' point. She even agreed with them. Nick couldn't expect her to stay in every night. And yet … and yet … she could imagine what he'd think when he heard she was out at a gig, mixing with pop stars and record company people. He'd be sure to imagine that the glamour would turn her head. It was just what he'd been afraid of…

But it's *not* the glamour, Becky thought rebelliously. There's nothing glamorous about Shaun. He's just a nice friendly guy who's interested in me and my life, and who happens to work for a music management company, that's all!

So here she was, on the 7.15 from Euston, heading home. Her parents had been delighted when she told them and Jan had promised a girls' get-together some time over the weekend.

And Nick?

Nick had sounded a bit strange. She'd rung him from the office, told him she was coming home, and hoped that he would offer to meet her train. But...

"What, this Friday?" he'd said, rather blankly.

"Yes," said Becky. "Why, is there a problem? You're not going away or anything, are you?"

There was a pause.

"No," he said. "No, I'll be here. Call me on Saturday morning, Becky. I'm looking forward to seeing you!"

Saturday morning, Becky thought, rather hurt. Why not Friday night? I wonder what he's doing? Maybe he's seeing someone else!

The thought gave her a definite stab of jealousy and left her feeling more confused than ever. I do love him, she thought. I must do, or I wouldn't mind the idea of him seeing another girl! But ... what about Shaun? Where does that leave him? Or me? Am I going to be torn between the two of them for ever?

The girls were right, she thought, folding up her magazine and gazing out of the carriage window. I've got to talk things over with Nick, find out where I stand. Her parents were waiting at the barrier when she got off the train. Little Emily was in her father's arms, half-asleep.

"She insisted on coming to meet you," her mum said, giving Becky a hug. "I knew it would be hopeless trying to get her to sleep, so we brought her along!"

"I want Becky to carry me!" wailed the little girl.

"You should be in bed, young lady," Becky said

as she tried to cuddle her little sister, hug her Dad, and hand in her ticket at the barrier, all at once! Oh, it's good to be home, she thought. I love the job, and the girls are great, and London's exciting but ... it's still good to be home!

She woke up early the next morning and for a split second wondered where she was. Then she yawned, and stretched, and smiled as she heard a tap on the door and her mum appeared with a mug of tea, Emily at her heels.

"Special treat!" Mrs Rivers laughed. "I bet nobody brings you tea in bed in the flat, do they?"

Becky shook her head, thinking of the usual early-morning chaos in the flat as the four of them – well, three usually, since Jade didn't work a nine-to-five day – struggled to be ready for work on time! Emily cuddled up beside her, threatening to make her spill her tea, and Mrs Rivers perched on the end of the bed.

"What are your plans, love? I expect you'll be seeing Jan, won't you? And ... Nick?"

Becky's heart lurched. I'll call Nick as soon as I get up, she thought. It's true, what the girls said. I won't really know how I feel until I see him again.

"I hope so," she said noncommittally. "But I haven't any real plans, Mum. I just came home to see you all!"

"And it's lovely to see you, Becky," beamed her mum. "We've missed you, love. Your dad and I were saying, it's just not the same at home these days. Not that we're not proud of you, mind! You've done really well!"

Becky got up, scrambled into her jeans and

sweatshirt, and went downstairs to the phone. Her throat felt dry and her fingers trembled as she dialled the familiar number.

"Nick? It's Becky!"

"Hi, Becky!" There was an awkward pause and Becky's heart began to thump. Was everything going to be all right? Was it?

"I thought we could ... er ... get together today," she said nervously.

"Yes, sure. Fine. Why don't you come round this morning?" said Nick.

And why don't you ask me out for tonight? Or have you got something better to do? thought Becky. But all she said was, "OK, I'll be round in about an hour!"

I don't believe this, she thought miserably, as she walked up the path to Nick's front door. It all looked just the same: the peeling front gate, the lace curtains at the windows, the rhododendron bushes. His house hasn't changed, Becky thought, but has Nick? Three months ago, I'd have popped round without thinking about it. I wouldn't have felt nervous at all. But now...

He must have been watching from the upstairs window because he opened the door before she rang the bell.

"Becky!"

"Oh, Nick!" She took a step forward, across the threshold, and fell into his arms. He held her, warmly, lovingly, against the rough wool of his sweater. She snuggled up close. Dear Nick, so familiar, so safe. He even smelled of the same aftershave.

"It's good to see you!" he said, smiling.

She looked up into his kind brown eyes. He'd had his hair cut since the weekend in London, quite short at the back, longer at the front. He wore a blue sweater and faded jeans and he was smiling at her in the same old way. Her heart leapt. I do love him, she thought. It's going to be all right...

"Come in," he said. "Everyone's out. Mum and Dad have gone shopping and Steve's taken Billy down to the Rec, so we've got the place to ourselves. Want a coffee?"

Becky sat in the living-room while Nick made coffee. Nothing's changed, she thought happily. Nick's just the same. All her doubts and fears seemed to have melted away now that she was back in the cosy, reassuring familiarity of Nick's front room.

"So how's London?" Nick said. "Sounds like you're having a good time, from your letters."

Was there just a tiny note of envy in his voice? I'm imagining it, Becky thought. "The job's great, Nick!" she said. "Oh, I did my very first pop interview last week, with a band called Rags..."

"Don't know them," said Nick.

"You won't, they're new," Becky went on. "I was so nervous, you wouldn't believe, but Paul, that's the singer, was so nice and friendly..."

"I bet he was," said Nick sarcastically.

Becky's smile faded. Oh, dear, she thought guiltily, I shouldn't be going on about pop stars; that's the last thing Nick wants to hear!

"Course, most of the time I'm in the office,

sorting out the post and filing the readers' letters," she went on hastily, to cover the awkward silence. "How about you? What are you doing? Your letters didn't tell me much..."

"Well, we can't all be brilliant letter-writers," said Nick sulkily. "As for what I'm doing, the answer is, not a lot. My uncle Joe, you know the one with the garage up on the bypass, says there's a job coming up delivering car spares. I quite fancy that, not being stuck in an office all day, getting out and about..."

"Nick, that's fantastic!" said Becky. "When will you know?"

"Next month, Joe says."

Silence fell again. Quick, thought Becky, what can I say? I don't want to sound big-headed, going on about the magazine and the music business all the time... "Do you see anything of Jan and the others?" she ventured.

"Not often. I don't go out clubbing much any more. Just to football, and out to the local with Des and Darren and all that crowd."

Poor Nick, Becky thought, it sounds boring! And who were Des and Darren? Pete Ransome had been Nick's best friend at school, but he'd gone to art college in Liverpool. Then Nick put down his coffee cup, turned to face her, and smiled in a way that melted her heart and turned her knees to water.

"I've missed you, Becky," he said huskily. "I've really missed you!"

His kiss was gentle, yet thrilling; familiar, yet carrying a hint of danger. It felt so good to be back in his arms, reminding Becky of the hundreds of kisses they must have shared since they first met. Of course he still loves me, she thought, as his arms tightened around her.

"Anyone home?" Mrs Miller, Nick's mum, put her head round the living-room door, and smiled as Nick and Becky sprang apart. Becky could see Nick's dad hovering in the hallway with several bags full of shopping.

"Hello, Becky, love! You're looking well, isn't she, Richard? How's life on that magazine of yours? I always look out for it in Smith's, you know!" Mrs Miller went on.

"Oh, I'm really enjoying it, thanks," Becky replied. Nick didn't say anything.

"You two going out tonight, then?" Mr Miller called.

"I … er…" Becky began, not knowing what to say. She had almost taken it for granted that she and Nick would be spending Saturday evening together. They still hadn't really talked, even though Nick was obviously pleased to see her and said he'd missed her. Perhaps we could have a quiet dinner for two in that new Italian restaurant Jan told me about, Becky thought.

"Yeah. Well," said Nick, "I'm going to a party, Becky. D'you want to come?"

"A party?" Becky echoed. It wasn't how she'd planned to spend her first evening with Nick for ages, but still…

"Yes, I'd love to!" she smiled, glad that she'd thought to pack her black dress with the handkerchief hem that Jade had told her was so sophisticated. "Whose party is it?"

"It's Darren's cousin's 18th," said Nick, "over on Windmill Lane. He's a real laugh, Becky, you'll like him. I'll pick you up at eight, OK?"

"OK," said Becky, glancing at her watch and seeing that it was almost one o'clock. "Mum's expecting me for lunch," she said. "I'll see you later!"

Nick saw her to the door and pulled her close to him for another passionate kiss as they said goodbye. He does still care, Becky thought, he must do...

Meeting Jan that afternoon for a Coke in the shopping centre was just like old times too. Jan soon filled her in on all the gossip about who was going out with whom, which couples had split up since school, which were the in pubs and clubs, what was happening.

"And what about you?" she said, when she finally drew breath. "Have you seen Nick yet? What did he say? Is everything still OK with you two?"

"Well, I think so," said Becky. "He hasn't really changed, Jan. He's talking about getting a job in his uncle's garage, delivering car spares."

"Is he taking you out tonight?" Jan demanded.

"Yes, we're going to a party. Someone's 18th, he said."

Jan raised her eyebrows. "I hadn't heard there were any parties going..."

"Over on Windmill Lane, he said."

Jan's eyes widened. "Not Jimmy Clark's place?"

"Who's Jimmy Clark?" asked Becky. "Nick said

it was ... ummm ... someone called Darren's cousin."

Jan nodded. "That's them," she said. "I'm surprised Nick knows them. They're trouble, that family!"

"He said they were a laugh," said Becky, worried. "Why, what have you heard, Jan? What's wrong with them?"

Jan looked uneasy. "Oh, nothing, probably," she said evasively. "Nick probably doesn't know them very well. And it may only be gossip, you know what this place is like! But Darren Clark's a bit wild, drives a flash car, that kind of thing; I wouldn't have thought he was Nick's type."

Becky thought, fleetingly, of Nick's friend Pete, the art student, who was shy and quiet and appealing, and his other friend Terry from the football team, whom she also liked very much. Neither of them could be described as "flash" in a million years.

"Well," she said slowly, "it's only a party! If we don't like the people, we can always leave."

All the same, she felt slightly uneasy as she dressed and made up for the party. When Nick arrived and she heard him chatting to her mum and dad downstairs, she gave herself a final spray of perfume and determinedly pushed Jan's gossip to the back of her mind.

Nick ushered her down the front path to a waiting car – not, to her surprise, a minicab, or even Steve's old van, but a big shiny Mercedes. He opened the rear door, and a blast of music hit her. A blonde girl with carefully-tousled hair, wearing a low-cut red satin top and white trousers, was already sitting there.

"This is my girlfriend, Becky," said Nick, as he slid into the front passenger seat. "Becky, this is Darren Clark, and..."

"I'm Mitzi," breathed the blonde girl in a little-girl voice that made Becky's hackles rise at once. She couldn't stand bimbos.

"Hi, Becky. Good to meet you!" said Darren, gunning the Mercedes' engine so that the car leapt forward with a squeal of brakes. Becky studied his face – what she could see of it – in the driver's mirror. He was older than Nick, in his mid-twenties she guessed, heavily-built, with a fleshy face and close-cropped dark hair. Not her type, but he seemed friendly enough.

There was no mistaking the house where the party was taking place! Every light was on, the drive was lined with parked cars, and the music was deafening. I'm not sure I'm going to enjoy this, Becky thought, as a drunken young man lurched past her, almost knocking her over, and she heard glass smashing and cheers coming from somewhere inside the house. Nick strode on ahead, through the front door, and there was nothing Becky could do but follow him. The party was certainly lively, with strobe lights, an entire disco sound-system with two DJs, and a seething mass of bodies either dancing or forcing their way to and from the bar.

"Coats upstairs!" a fair-haired girl in a red dress bawled at her over the steady thump of the music. Becky dumped her coat, combed her hair, and tried to spot Nick in the crush. She was beginning to feel thoroughly cross. Nick must've known what it would be like, she thought. I'll be lucky if I even get to dance with him at this rate, never mind talk to him! I don't know anyone here, and from the state of most of them, I'm not sure that I want to!

Where *was* Nick? Oh, there he was, emerging from the kitchen with a can of lager and a plastic cup which he handed to her.

"OK, Becky? Come along in and have a dance," he urged.

The music was so loud it was impossible to talk. In fact, it was almost impossible to move in the living-room. Becky sipped her not-very-nice white wine with a shudder. She'd rather have had a refreshing Coke...

"It's a bit crowded..." she objected.

"Sorry, what was that?" yelled Nick.

"I SAID IT'S A BIT CROWDED!" Becky roared back.

Nick forced his way over to the other side of the room where there was more space. The DJ changed the record to a George Michael ballad, much to Becky's relief. Nick slipped his arms round her waist and she rested her face against his chest. This is more like it, she thought dreamily, as they swayed gently together. She looked up at him and the expression in his eyes told her everything she had longed to know. How could I have thought he didn't care any more? she thought guiltily. Of course he cares. Didn't he introduce me to Darren and that silly Mitzi as his girlfriend? Everything's the same, everything's still the same...

"Fancy another drink, Becky? It's so hot in here!" Nick murmured.

"Could I have a Coke or something? That wine was horrible!" Becky replied.

"OK."

Nick threaded his way through the crowd and Becky went over to the French windows, which someone had just opened. She stepped out on to the patio and let the night air cool her hot face. Her head was beginning to ache and she half-wished she could ask Nick to take her home, or at least somewhere quieter. This isn't my kind of party, she thought, as she heard a burst of raucous laughter, and these aren't my kind of people...

"All alone, little lady?" said a voice, making her jump. She turned to see a scruffy-looking guy in torn jeans and a leather biker's jacket coming towards her. As he drew nearer she smelt drink on his breath. Alarm prickled up the back of her neck and she stepped back towards the safety of the house.

"Don't run away, beautiful. That's not nice. Not friendly!" he said, reaching out and grabbing her wrist in a grip that hurt.

"Let go!" said Becky, twisting away and trying not to panic. Where was Nick? Where was everyone? Were they all so busy dancing and drinking in there that they couldn't see what was going on on the patio, just a few feet away?

"Don't be like that!" he said, pulling her towards him.

"Leave me alone!" yelled Becky, shoving him away with all her strength. But somehow, he dodged around until he was between her and the French windows, and safety.

"Oh, no, you don't," he snarled. "Not without giving me a little kiss!"

He grabbed her again.

"Nick!" Becky yelled, scratching and struggling.

"What's going on here?" demanded Nick angrily. Becky wrenched herself free from the biker's grasp and fled into the living-room, gasping and sobbing. Miraculously, the crowd parted to let her through. She was dimly aware of a commotion behind her ... raised voices, a girl's scream, the sound of breaking glass, but all she wanted to do was get away, fetch her coat and bag, then find Nick and go home.

"What happened?" asked the blonde in the red dress who had showed her where to put her coat. "I'm Diane, Jim's girlfriend. Are you all right? You're shivering. Here, put this round you!"

"I ... I'm all right," said Becky, with an effort. "There was a guy on the patio ... I think he'd had too much to drink..."

She found her coat at last and slipped it on. Diane patted her arm. It was cool and quiet upstairs but Becky could still hear shrieks and thumps above the relentless thud of the music. Oh, God, she thought, I hope Nick's all right...

She sprang to her feet. "My boyfriend!" she cried wildly. "I've got to go down, make sure he's all right!"

As Becky reached the top of the stairs there was

another almighty crash. She gazed down in horror. Three or four men, Nick's friend Darren among them, were manhandling the guy in the leather jacket along the hallway. He was yelling and swearing, flailing out with his arms and legs, knocking over plants, pictures, a small table…

Someone opened the front door and he was flung out on to the gravel drive, still shouting.

Oh, no, Becky thought, terrified. Where's Nick? What's happened to him? Did they have a fight? I shouldn't have left him, run off like that…

She flew down the stairs, stumbling in her party sandals. Someone had turned the music off and the guests were standing around, looking awkward. A couple of the girls were crying. Mitzi's pretty, doll-like face was streaked with mascara and tears.

"Nick?" Becky whispered.

He lay on the sofa, as white as a ghost, his eyes closed and a trickle of blood in the corner of his mouth. Becky stared at him in horror.

"N … Nick?" she repeated. Someone put a comforting arm round her.

"He just got himself into a bit of bother," said a soothing voice. "Don't worry, love, I'm sure he'll be all right. We've phoned for an ambulance…"

"Ambulance," Becky echoed. This is a nightmare, she thought. It can't be happening. I'll wake up, any moment, and find that it isn't true.

And then she heard the wail of a siren in the distance…

8

"**B**ut what happened?" gasped Jan.

It was Sunday afternoon, and she and Becky were up in Becky's room, talking over the events of the previous night. Becky felt weepy and exhausted. It had been after three when her dad drove her home from the hospital.

"Oh, Jan," she said in a shaky voice, "it … it was awful! I … I truly thought Nick was dead!"

Jan put a comforting arm round her. "He's going to be all right, though, isn't he? You said on the phone…"

Becky nodded. "Yes, he's going to be fine. Mild concussion, the doctor said. They were going to keep him in hospital overnight and let him go home today. I shall call in and see him when Dad drives me to the station this evening."

"Well, then," said Jan soothingly, "there's no real harm done!"

Becky's eyes filled with tears. It was a relief to know that Nick wasn't seriously hurt. But every time she thought of him lying on that sofa, so white and still, she went cold inside. It could have been so much worse.

"I keep thinking it was my fault..." she said hesitantly.

"Your fault? How could it be?" Jan demanded.

"Well, Nick was defending me", Becky argued, "from that awful drunk. I ... I screamed and panicked, Jan. If I'd kept calm ... or not run away when Nick turned up, maybe I could've ... could've stopped him, stopped them fighting. Or something..."

Her voice trailed off into silence.

"I never heard anything so idiotic," said Jan briskly. "Of course it wasn't your fault! Some horrible drunk starts pawing you at a party and you get scared. Any girl would have! And as for stopping the fight, didn't you say it took three of them to throw the guy out in the end? He was obviously dying to have a go at someone, and Nick happened to get in the way. It was *his* fault, Becky, no one else's! You mustn't blame yourself, not for a moment!"

Becky sniffed and blew her nose. She knew, deep down inside, that Jan was right. But she couldn't bear the idea of Nick, her gentle, laid-back, non-violent Nick, getting hurt trying to defend her. He had always said that he wasn't the hero type, that he'd walk away from any trouble. But when she needed him, he'd been there for her, standing up to some tough drunken biker for her sake...

"If it comes to that," said Jan, "Nick should've

117

known better than to take you to a party like that anyway! He might have known there'd be trouble!"

Becky's dad had said much the same thing on the way back from the hospital, but Becky hadn't expected to hear it from Jan too!

"Well, thanks a bunch," she said sarcastically. "How on earth was Nick supposed to know what would happen? That biker was a gate-crasher anyway, Diane said!" She glared at her friend.

Jan patted her arm. "OK, OK, keep your hair on. Nick's a hero, a knight in shining armour. Don't worry, Becky, he'll be OK in a day or two."

"But I'll be back in London then," said Becky forlornly.

And I shall want to forget all about this weekend, she thought. Seeing her family, and Jan and Nick, had been all right, but that hot, crowded, noisy party, the drunken biker, the arrival of the ambulance, the trip to the Accident and Emergency department in Diane's car, the anxious wait at the hospital for her dad and Nick's parents, the relief when a harassed young doctor told them that Nick had regained consciousness and wasn't badly hurt, her dad's arms round her as she sobbed with relief, Nick's mum's white, frightened face... No, she wanted to forget all that.

"I can't wait to come and see you and check out this flat I've heard so much about," grinned Jan. "I'll be able to do my Christmas shopping in Oxford Street and Covent Garden! It's been lovely seeing you, Becky. Don't even think about last night any more. It was nasty but it's over, and Nick's going to be fine."

"I suppose so," said Becky with a sigh.

When the time came for her to leave, her mum looked worried and gave her an extra-long hug. "I wish you could stay until tomorrow, love," she murmured. "Couldn't you ring your boss and explain?"

Becky was tempted, but in the end she shook her head. They were very busy at work, and it would mean changing her weekend train ticket, and anyway, she told herself, what good would it do?

It was all she could do not to burst into tears again when she saw Nick. He was pale and quiet, and if her dad and Nick's family hadn't been around she would have flung herself into his arms and cried.

"How are you feeling?" she asked him tenderly.

"OK," he said, "except for a headache! Don't worry about me, Becky!"

"The police have been round," said Mrs Miller, "but Nick absolutely refuses to press charges. I think he should, don't you, Becky? Goodness, he could have been killed!"

"Oh, Mum, we've been through all that!" Nick snapped. "It was nothing!"

"Nothing? I supposed that's why you ended up in hospital, frightening us all to death," said Mr Miller. "See if you can talk some sense into him, Becky. He won't listen to a word I say!"

"Oh, Nick," said Becky helplessly. She knew how stubborn Nick could be.

"But there was nothing to it!" said Nick,

sounding more irritable than ever. "I told you, Dad. This guy was hassling Becky, I told him to leave her alone, he gave me a shove, I tripped and hit my head on the edge of the patio doors, that was all. It wasn't a fight. The guy probably didn't mean to hurt me."

Becky remembered the swearing, struggling biker she'd seen thrown out of the house. "He looked like a maniac to me!" she objected.

Nick shrugged. "Lay off, Becky, will you?" he snapped. "As far as I'm concerned it was an accident. It's over, and I'm fine. I don't know why you can't all just leave me alone!"

Becky felt as though he had hit her. Mrs Miller put an arm round her.

"I think you should apologize, Nick," she said, gently but firmly. "Becky's just worried about you. We all are! She's come round to see how you are and say goodbye. There's no need to be rude!"

Nick looked up, and then smiled reluctantly, looking much more like his old self. "I'm sorry, Becky, OK?" he said. "I'll see you next time you come up. And I'll write, I promise!"

He's just bad-tempered and cross because his head hurts, Becky told herself, as she gave him a gentle kiss on the cheek and said goodbye.

It was only when she was sitting in the train speeding back towards London that she remembered that she and Nick still hadn't really talked...

Ruth and Fi were at home when she got back to Camberwell. Jade was out with her boyfriend.

"Hi. Want a cuppa?" said Fi breezily as Becky walked in. Then, as she caught sight of her face, she said, "Oh, dear, as bad as that, was it?"

"Yes. Well ... no, not the way you mean," said Becky, feeling as though all she wanted to do was fall into bed and sleep for a week.

"So is it all on with Nick, or off?" Ruth wanted to know.

"On. At least, I think so. He took me to a party and got himself knocked down when some ghastly drunk tried it on with me," said Becky wearily.

"You poor thing!" Fi said. "Why don't you go and have a nice hot bath? Ruth and I will make some cocoa, and I think there are some Jaffa cakes in the tin!"

By the time Becky had had her bath, Jade had come in. Sipping her cocoa gratefully, Becky related the story of her disastrous weekend.

"Poor old Becky," said Fi. "You must have been terrified."

"Yes, and the worst thing was, I sort of blamed myself," groaned Becky. "If I hadn't panicked when the biker came towards me..."

"Just as well you did," said Fi indignantly. "I'd have screamed blue murder!"

"But Nick's going to be all right, that's the main thing," Ruth said sympathetically. Becky couldn't suppress an enormous yawn.

"I'm *so* tired," she complained. "It was all horrible, and I hardly got any sleep last night, and Nick was so grumpy this afternoon when I went to see him..."

"It'll all look different in the morning," Fi

promised. "Go to bed, Becky. Get yourself a decent night's kip and you'll feel better."

Becky did feel better in the morning. I'm going to forget about that party, she thought. I'm going to remember the good things about the weekend, like how lovely it was to see Nick again, how he held me, how he kissed me. Of course he still loves me. Didn't he say he'd missed me?

Going back to work helped, too. Almost the first thing Linda said to her when she arrived in the office was, "Becky, I really liked the way you wrote up that Rags interview. Well done!"

So much seemed to have happened in the last few days that Becky had to think for a moment before she could even remember the Rags interview!

"Thanks, Linda," she said, feeling a thrill of pride. Her first-ever pop interview, and Linda liked it!

"I was sent a press release this morning about a seventeen-year-old girl who has just made her first record," Linda went on. "I wondered if you'd like to interview her, Becky, not as a pop feature, but more along the lines of what it's like for a young girl straight from school to be catapulted into the music business?"

"I'd love to," said Becky, glancing at the publicity photo. An idea suddenly occurred to her. "Linda?" she began, rather shyly.

"Yes?"

"I wonder ... could we make it into a little series, on young girls in exciting jobs? I could interview this singer, an actress, a model, a ballet dancer..."

Linda clapped her hands. "That's a *great* idea, Becky! Not big stars or top names, just hard-working young people trying to make it into the big-time."

"My flatmate Jade is a model," Becky added. "She spends hours and hours trailing around London with her model book, and as often as not she doesn't get the job."

"Better and better. We want to show what working life is really like for these people," said Linda. "OK, Becky, that can be your next project!"

Becky settled down at her desk, feeling excited. A series of my own! she thought.

She was soon brought down to earth when she saw the huge pile of letters to be opened and filed. The telephone rang on and off all morning too, so she was far too busy to think about her love-life.

She was just about to shut down her computer and take a well-deserved lunch break when the phone rang again. She was tempted to let it ring, but in the end she picked it up, hoping it wouldn't be anything important or complicated.

"Becky?" said a familiar voice. "It's Shaun! Shaun Carswell!"

Becky was so startled that she almost dropped the phone. Her hands began to shake and there was a strange hollow feeling in the pit of her stomach.

"Oh ... hello, Shaun..." she said weakly.

"I'm really sorry that I haven't called you before," he went on, "but I had to go off on the road with one of our bands. I've been thinking about you, though..."

"H – have you?" echoed Becky.

"Yes. Paul told me that you'd interviewed him and that he'd really enjoyed it. Did you get everything you wanted?"

Keep calm, Becky thought, this is obviously just a business call. "Yes, thanks. I enjoyed it too," she managed to say coolly. "This morning my boss told me she really liked the piece I wrote!"

"She did? Congratulations, Becky!" said Shaun. She could hear the warmth in his voice. He was obviously really pleased for her. Oh, he is nice, she thought, I do like him...

Shaun was still speaking and she heard him say something about "celebration".

"Sorry," she said, "I didn't quite catch that. Celebrating what?"

"'Rags' single is at Number 37 in the Top Forty!" said Shaun. "I've just been given a pay rise, and your boss is pleased with you. I said, we ought to go out and celebrate!"

Becky's stomach lurched. So it wasn't just business after all. Shaun wanted to see her, take her out. What can I say? she thought. I would like to see him again, I really would. But there's Nick...

"Becky?" Shaun was saying. "Are you still there? I know a nice little Thai restaurant not far from your place..."

"Thai?" said Becky faintly.

"Yes, have you ever tried Thai food? If you're free tomorrow night, I'll book us a table."

Suddenly, Becky came to life. Yes, she thought, I will go out with Shaun tomorrow night. It's just like the girls said, I've got to have a social life down here. Nick can't expect me to stay in every night. But I shall tell Shaun I've got a boyfriend at home and that he and I can only ever be friends. That's what I'll do. That way, everyone will know just where they are.

"That sounds great, Shaun," she said, happy to have found a simple solution to her dilemma. There was no reason, no reason at all, why she and Shaun couldn't be friends. Platonic, wasn't that the word? When you got on well with someone, and enjoyed their company, but you both knew there was absolutely no chance of any romance developing between you...

"So, if you and Shaun are just friends, why are you prowling around like a cat on hot bricks?" Fi demanded the next night, after Becky had been to the loo twice, checked her make-up three times, and changed her mind yet again about what she was going to wear.

The front doorbell rang before Becky could reply. She froze.

"Quick," she hissed, "where did I put my bag? And where's my coat? Keys … keys, I've lost my keys! Fi, could you buzz down to Shaun and tell him I won't be a minute?"

Giggling wildly, Fi passed on the message. A few moments later, a very flustered Becky careered down the stairs, wishing her heart wasn't hammering quite so hard.

"Hi, Becky!" Shaun kissed her on the cheek and stood back to admire her almost-new green velvet dress. "Wow!" he said simply.

He led her down the path towards the shabbiest old car she had ever seen. He opened the door for her and she scrambled over a pile of newspapers to sit down.

"Excuse the transport," said Shaun, grinning. "I share this old rust-heap with my brother. He's got his own painting-and-decorating business, that's why it pongs a bit of paint. I hope you don't mind?"

"Not at all," said Becky, relaxing at once. There's nothing to be nervous about, she thought. I'd forgotten how comfortable I feel with Shaun!

The car clattered through the London streets, sounding as though it was at its last gasp. Becky suddenly remembered Nick's bitter words about her being driven around London in a Ferrari by some media type, and almost giggled. How wrong can you be, she thought.

Thai food turned out to be just as delicious as Shaun had promised, full of subtle, spicy, lemony flavours.

"I'm so pleased about Rags' single, Shaun," she told him, over coffee.

"I know. It's good news, isn't it?" Shaun replied. "The band were over the moon, you can imagine! They've worked really hard, they deserve to make it. And talking of making it..."

Her hand was lying on the table. He put his over it, and squeezed. "You're doing very well, too, aren't you?" he said, smiling.

Should I snatch my hand away, Becky thought, or will I look like a prude? I've got to tell him about Nick some time...

"Er ... yes," she began. "And Linda's given me another interesting project to work on, Shaun..."

"That's wonderful!" he said, beaming at her. "I bet you can't wait to see your name in print, can you?"

Becky laughed and shook her head. Across the candlelit table, her eyes met Shaun's. What she saw in those greeny-hazel depths made her swallow hard and look away. *Tell him*, said the voice of her conscience. *Tell him about Nick!*

"Er ... Shaun?" she began.

"Yes?"

"I went home last weekend..."

"Did you?"

"Er ... yes. To see my mum and dad, and my best friend. And ... er ... my boyfriend!" Shaun's expression was unreadable.

"Boyfriend?" he queried gently.

"Yes. Nick. We've ... we've been together since school."

"That's nice," said Shaun blandly.

Oh, help, Becky thought, I'm doing this all wrong! Perhaps Shaun doesn't even fancy me, perhaps he just thinks of me as a friend anyway.

"Becky," said Shaun gently, "what are you trying to say?"

She could see the candle flame reflected in his eyes. He looked very serious, and very attractive, and extremely fanciable. I must be crazy, Becky thought. How can Shaun and I just be friends, when he makes me feel like this? Perhaps I ought to finish it completely?

"I ... I..." she stammered.

"You're trying to tell me that you don't want to see me again, because of this guy at home," said Shaun.

"No!" Becky cried, so loudly that a couple at the next table turned to stare.

"No?"

"No ... I'm sorry, Shaun ... what I mean is ... I really like you, but I want us just to be friends," she managed to stammer.

"Friends," Shaun echoed, his face expressionless.

"Mmm." Becky nodded vigorously, wishing she sounded more convincing. It *is* what I want, she told herself firmly. Shaun looked up at her, smiling, and her heart skipped a beat.

"OK," he said easily, "friends it is. Whatever you want, Becky!"

"You mean ... you mean you don't mind?" she faltered, not sure whether she was relieved or offended.

His smile widened. "Friends is absolutely fine," he assured her. "I really like you, too, Becky. And I can always use another friend. Can't everyone?"

"Well ... yes," said Becky, uncertainly. Why am I disappointed? she thought to herself. Did I really want Shaun to stamp off into the night swearing that he couldn't live without me? He's agreed to be friends. That's great. Isn't it?

When Shaun dropped her at the flat with a gentle kiss on the cheek, she watched the taillight of his battered old car disappear down the street with a pang of longing. What's the matter with me? she thought. I've done the right thing...

Nick kept his promise and wrote her a letter

which arrived at the end of the week. Becky opened it with shaking fingers, but it turned out to be just like Nick's other letters – short, to the point, and not in the least romantic. He told her he was feeling much better. His headache had gone. He was almost sure he'd get the job in his uncle's garage. He was looking forward to being able to play football again next week. He did sign it "lots of love, Nick" and there were a whole row of kisses under his name, but it wasn't exactly what you'd call a love-letter, Becky decided.

She also had a card from Jan, full of excitement about coming down for the weekend.

"It's OK, isn't it, if my old schoolfriend comes to stay? She says she doesn't mind sleeping on the sofa!" said Becky to her flatmates on Sunday.

"Better than that, she can have my bed. Ben's taking me home for the weekend," said Jade, licking marmalade off her fingers. "What are you doing, Christmas shopping?"

"Yes. I can't believe Christmas is only five weeks away," said Becky. "I haven't bought a single thing yet. I'd like to take Jan out clubbing on Saturday night, or to a party or something."

Fi sat up straight. "Why don't we have a party here? Nothing fancy, just a few wine boxes and some French bread and cheese and dips and things? I'm sure some of the gang from work would come, and we could ask the girls from downstairs..."

"That's a wonderful idea, Fi!" said Ruth. "I'm sure my friends from work would come, and there's my brother and his pals from the office.

Yes, let's! People get bored with Christmas parties, so let's get ours in early."

"Invite your mate Shaun too, Becky," Fi insisted. "He works in the music business, doesn't he? Get him to bring a few tasty pop stars along!"

Becky joined in the general laughter, but she couldn't help worrying. Should she invite Shaun? He hadn't rung her, but they'd agreed to be friends, and what could be friendlier than inviting him to a party?

When Shaun finally did call her, in the office on Monday, he said he'd be delighted to come. "Sounds fun. I'll see you on Saturday night then, shall I? About eight?" he said, sounding as relaxed and as casual as ever.

She met Jan off the train on Saturday morning, and took her to Covent Garden where they shopped till they dropped, or nearly!

"Oh, my poor feet!" gasped Jan, loaded down with carrier-bags. "Let's go and have a coffee or something, Becky!"

Becky led the way to a nearby café and the two girls sank thankfully into the nearest seats.

"Have you heard from Nick?" Jan demanded.

"Yes, he wrote to me. I think he's OK," said Becky. "I did try phoning once, but there was no reply."

Jan toyed with her plastic teaspoon. "Becky..." she began.

"Yes?"

"Look," Jan said awkwardly, "I don't know how to tell you this, in fact I don't even know whether I should tell you at all..."

Becky's smile faded. "Whatever is it?" she asked.

"You know Darren Clark? Nick's friend?"

Becky shivered, remembering the awful night of the party and Darren, with his flash car and silly blonde girlfriend. "What about him?"

"He and his brother are in trouble with the law," Jan said. "Serious trouble, from what I hear. I don't know what it is they're supposed to have done – some fraud, or swindle, or something..."

"Oh, are they?" said Becky coldly. Jan seemed to have it in for Nick's friends, for some reason.

Jan shrugged impatiently. "What I'm saying is, those guys are strictly bad news, Becky. Nick doesn't want to get mixed up with them, honestly. Why don't you have a word, next time you talk to him?"

Becky sighed. "What could I say? I don't even know them! And I can't tell him where to go or who to see, anyway, can I?"

Jan shrugged again. "Well, don't say you haven't been warned," she said.

With an effort, Becky pushed the thought of Nick and his problems to the back of her mind. Perhaps, when she next spoke to him, she would say something. But would he listen?

The two girls caught a bus down to Camberwell, where they discovered Ruth baking quiches and Fi mixing salad. Becky and Jan went out shopping for wine, French bread and cheese, and then Jan volunteered to mix her famous avocado dip while Becky tidied the living-room, replacing the glaring central lighting with everyone's bedside lamps to give a party feel to the room.

"Not bad, is it?" she said proudly, when everything was ready. Jan was wandering round with her hair in heated rollers and Fi was painting her toenails while Ruth had a bath. Somehow, in spite of the chaos, they were all dressed and made-up by the time the first guests started arriving.

Becky was struggling to open a wine box in the kitchen when Jan almost fell into the room, her eyes wide with excitement. "The most gorgeous guy has just arrived!" she hissed. "You've got to introduce me!"

Becky looked up from the wine box, hot, cross and flustered. "Gorgeous guy?" she said. "He's probably one of Ruth's friends, I don't know…"

"Hi, Becky!" came a familiar voice from the doorway.

It was Shaun.

9

"D'you need any help with that? Looks like you're having trouble!" said Shaun cheerfully, striding across the kitchen and opening the wine box with a flick of one strong, male wrist.

"Thanks, Shaun," said Becky gratefully. Her heart was still thumping. A gorgeous guy, Jan had said. Shaun *was* looking good, in a cream shirt and pale fawn chinos. Perhaps Jan did fancy him. Why shouldn't she? He and Becky were just friends, after all...

"It was nothing. All you need is a bit of muscle power, and masculine know-how!" teased Shaun.

"Don't tell me we've invited a male chauvinist to our party!" said Fi, coming in and helping herself to a glass of wine.

"Shaun finally managed to open the wine box. I'd been struggling with it for ages," Becky put in.

"Oh, well, guys have their uses!" laughed Fi, wandering back towards the living-room. Becky took a deep breath and said, "Jan, this is my friend Shaun Carswell. Jan's a friend from home, Shaun. We went to school together; she's doing a secretarial course now."

"I'm hoping to get a job in London when I get my diploma," said Jan eagerly. Becky watched them chatting with a sinking heart. They seemed to get on really well. She does fancy him, she thought despondently. As for Shaun, it was hard to tell how he felt. What's the matter with me? Becky thought. I've got Nick. Shaun's just a friend, someone I go out with from time to time. I should be glad that he and Jan like each other...

Suddenly, this party didn't seem like such a good idea after all. Shaun and Jan were still deep in conversation. I ought to leave them to it, Becky thought gloomily, go and see who's in the living-room, maybe have a dance.

She had never felt less like dancing in her life. Instead, she busied herself getting out a few more glasses and opening some extra packets of crisps.

"I might have known!" said a familiar Scottish voice. "Sneaking off into the kitchen with the two best-looking babes at the party, Carswell! Why don't you give the rest of us a chance?"

Becky swung round in surprise. It was Paul, lead singer with Rags, looking every inch the rock star in tight black leather trousers and a skinny T-shirt which clung to his rangy body.

"Oh... Paul, I forgot about you!" said Shaun guiltily.

Paul raised one eyebrow and laughed. "I can see why!" he said.

Shaun turned to Becky. "You don't mind me

134

bringing Paul, do you?" he asked anxiously. "I know I should've called you and checked that it was OK, but we've had such a hectic week..."

"Of course I don't mind," said Becky, smiling. "It's nice to see you again, Paul! Shaun told me about the single going in at 37. I'm so pleased for you!"

"Not bad, is it, for a first go?" said Paul. "I came down here for a business meeting yesterday. I'm sleeping on Shaun's sofa."

"Shaun's sofa? Won't the record company pay for a hotel?" said Becky, bewildered. She had always imagined that pop singers with recording contracts were rolling in money.

Paul made a face. "Well, they probably would, but it would all have to come out of our advance," he said ruefully. "They've spent thousands on us already, Becky, what with equipment and recording costs and touring and the video and everything. None of us will get a penny of it back until we start selling a few records!"

"He won't be splashing out on a Porsche or luxury yacht just yet!" said Shaun. Becky burst out laughing. Then she suddenly became aware of Jan, who was looking at Paul as though she had never seen a guy before. A huge weight seemed to float away from Becky's shoulders. It's Paul Jan fancies, not Shaun, she thought, with a sudden flash of insight. She must have spotted him in the living-room and come in to ask me who he was! She's not interested in Shaun after all! She felt so relieved she could have hugged Jan. Instead, she gave her an encouraging smile.

"Sorry, Jan," she said, "I should've introduced you! This is Paul Maclean, who sings with a band called Rags. I interviewed him for the magazine a few weeks ago..."

"Hi, Jan. Nice to meet you," said Paul's caressing voice. Becky saw the way they were looking at each other, and smiled to herself. That's Jan fixed up, she thought cheerfully, and with a real live pop star too! Even if he doesn't ask for her phone number, it'll give Jan an evening to remember! Meanwhile...

"How about a dance, Becky?" said Shaun

It was the best party she had been to since ... well, ever since she could remember, Becky thought, as she and Shaun moved and swayed in time with the music. No one was drunk, no one was aggressive, everyone was having a good time. The music made you want to dance, the wine flowed, and everyone had praised Ruth's quiches and Jan's avocado dip!

Best of all, there was Shaun; laughing, joking, teasing, and just listening to her. They never seemed to run out of things to say to one another and she always felt he was interested in her. He wasn't the sort of guy who talked about himself all the time. He didn't leave her in a corner of the room with a drink and a bag of peanuts while he discussed football or cars with his mates, as Nick, she had to admit, had sometimes done. Oh dear, thought Becky guiltily, I shouldn't be thinking like that! I love Nick, and he loves me. Only a couple of weeks ago he was fighting another guy for my sake...

But Nick seemed a very long way away, so did that other disastrous party. There won't be any fights this time, she thought as she and Shaun took a break from dancing to talk to Ruth, her brother, and a French friend of his, who looked like Eric Cantona and spoke very little English.

"You like a sheep?" he asked Becky.

"A *sheep*?" repeated Becky blankly, looking round as though she expected a flock of them to come baa-ing through the door. Shaun started to laugh, indicating the dish that Pierre was holding.

"I think he means a chip! A potato crisp!" he said.

"*Mais oui!* A cheep. A creesp!" said Pierre, not at all offended. "Excuse my bad English; I learn, onlee!"

"It's better than my French!" giggled Becky.

"*Tu parles français, alors?*" said the young Frenchman.

"Er ... *non*. Not really. *Un petit peu* ... a little!"

"A leetle is good. And you?" he went on, waving a hand at Shaun.

"Not at all," said Shaun, looking serious for once. "All I can say in French is '*Je t'aime*'. That means 'I love you', doesn't it?"

Pierre nodded, and Becky looked away, feeling flustered. It didn't mean anything, she was sure, so why was she so unwilling to meet Shaun's eyes? They'd been having such a good time, why did he have to spoil it by getting romantic? Or was she just imagining the whole thing?

"Come on, Shaun! Fi, Pierre ... Ruth! Let's all

have a dance!" she cried gaily. But when the
music slowed down, and Whitney Houston sang a
romantic ballad, and Shaun's arms went round
her waist, she didn't pull away.

"I've really enjoyed tonight, Becky," he murmured against her hair.

"So have I," she replied truthfully.

She looked up, met his eyes, and felt as though
she was drowning in their greeny-hazel depths.
Just friends, her head was telling her, but her
heart said something quite different. Her head
said that Shaun was a friend, her heart insisted
that he was someone she could love...

Oh, it's hopeless, Becky thought, pulling away
abruptly. I *can't* just be friends with him, he's too
... too... Attractive? Nice? Sexy? She didn't know.
Shaun was all those things, and more besides. He
was funny, and sweet, and intelligent, and
everything any girl could want in a boyfriend.

Except that he wasn't her boyfriend. Nick was.

"Becky? What's the matter?" Shaun was looking
troubled.

Becky managed to smile. "Oh, it's nothing," she
said. "I was just ... I don't know, I think I'm a bit
tired. Jan and I did some of our Christmas
shopping today."

"Oh, don't," he groaned, "I haven't bought anything yet! What are you doing for Christmas,
Becky?"

"Going home," said Becky, surprised that he
should ask. "It was wonderful last year. My baby
sister really believes in Father Christmas!"

"Of course she does!" said Shaun, in mock

surprise. "Doesn't everyone? You're not trying to tell me … Becky! You're not trying to tell me that Father Christmas isn't a real person?"

Becky giggled. "You are a clown!" she told him affectionately, relieved that the difficult moment seemed to have passed.

Shaun and Paul left at about half-past one in the morning, Paul with Jan's phone number in his trouser pocket. Shaun gave Becky a gentle kiss on the lips as he left. "Bye, Becky," he said softly. "It was a great party! I'll give you a call soon, then maybe we can go out to a gig or something."

"That would be lovely," said Becky, trying to smile. It had only been a little kiss, the kind a guy might give to a good friend. Yet Becky could still feel the gentle pressure of his lips on hers.

Shaun's car wheezed and rattled out into the main road while she and Jan stood waving at the front door. Then they went inside.

"Well," said Jan, stretching like a satisfied cat, "that was quite a party!"

Becky laughed. "I'm glad you enjoyed it. Paul's nice, isn't he?"

"Gorgeous," said Jan simply. "I don't suppose he'll call me, guys like that never do, but he did give me his manager's number, and said that when they're playing in our area I was to call and he'd put me on the band's guest list! That was nice of him, wasn't it?"

"Very nice," said Becky. "You should go and see them anyway, Jan. They're ever so good! Catch them on their next tour, while they're still playing small clubs!"

"I might just do that," said Jan, as the two girls went into the living-room. The party was coming to an end. Ruth was talking to her brother and a couple of his friends, and Fi was clearing away some empty glasses.

The next morning, Becky was woken up just before ten by the insistent shrilling of the telephone.

"All right, all right, I'm coming!" she called, scrabbling under the bed for her slippers. Fi, in the other bed, was still dead to the world.

"Becky? Is that you?" came Nick's voice. Becky's heart jumped into her throat and she felt wide awake at once. "I didn't wake you, did I?"

"Doesn't matter. It's time I woke up, anyway. What a nice surprise, Nick!" said Becky.

"Well, Mum and Dad are still in bed, so I thought I'd call."

"How are you? No more headaches?"

"Oh no, I'm fine." There was still a trace of impatience in his tone.

"Jan's down this weekend. We've ... er ... we've been Christmas shopping!" Becky told him.

"Oh, yes? And out clubbing, I bet! No wonder you're only half-awake!" said Nick. Becky felt a pang of guilt.

"No, we didn't got out clubbing, We ... we ... er ... had some friends round," she said. Now, why didn't I say it was a party? she asked herself. There seems to be so much I can't say to Nick these days! Not just about Shaun, but about work, or pop interviews, or having a good time, in case he thinks I'm being flash! Why do boys have to be so touchy, anyway?

"Sounds fun."

"It was. One of Ruth's French friends asked me if I liked sheep!"

"*Sheep?*"

"That's what I thought he said," Becky went on, starting to giggle again. "But it turned out he was offering me a chip, you know, a crisp!"

Nick didn't laugh. Oh, well, thought Becky, perhaps it was one of those jokes you had to be there to appreciate.

"How's the family?" she said. "Looking forward to Christmas?"

"S'pose so," said Nick. "You are coming home, aren't you, Becky?"

"Of course I'm coming home, silly," said Becky, "where else would I go?"

"Well … I just thought you might be staying in London…" Nick sounded so humble that Becky immediately felt sorry for him. Poor old Nick, she thought; it can't be much fun for him, stuck up there, jobless and broke, while I tell him about all the fun I'm having!

"I'm looking forward to seeing you," she said gently.

"Look, I've got to go," said Nick. "I'll talk to you soon, OK? Take care!"

"Who was that on the phone?" yawned Jan, coming out of the other bedroom in a dressing-gown she'd borrowed from Ruth.

"Nick."

Jan giggled. "He must have a sixth sense," she

said, "phoning you the day after you've seen Shaun! Still, what the eye doesn't see, the heart doesn't grieve over, as my Nan used to say."

"It's not like that," said Becky with dignity. "I told you, Jan. Shaun and I are just good friends."

She could see from Jan's expression that her friend didn't believe her.

"If I were you," Jan said bluntly, as they sat in the kitchen with big mugs of coffee, "I'd dump Nick right away. Shaun's far more your type. He's bright, he's lively, he's ambitious, he's in the same business. Face it, Becky, Nick Miller's a complete loser!"

"Jan!" gasped Becky, feeling rather as though a bucket of cold water had been thrown over her. "He is not!"

"Yes, he is!" Jan said. "Look at him. First, he fails his exams. OK, that can happen to anyone, but anyone else would've picked himself up and started over by now! And what has Nick done? Just mucked about at home for months, getting mixed up with the Clarks and their dodgy crowd..."

"That's not fair!" snapped Becky. "You've never liked Nick! You always used to call him a wimp..."

"He is a wimp!" Jan snapped back.

"No, he's not!" cried Becky heatedly. "Would a wimp have rescued me from that awful biker?"

"You shouldn't have been there!" said Jan stubbornly. "Everyone in town knows the Clarks are trouble."

"Oh, I don't know, Jan," Becky said hopelessly. "I do like Shaun, of course I do. But Nick and I go back a long way. We always thought we'd stay together after school. And ... and when I left home, he ... he said he was sure I'd end up with some flash media type in a Ferrari..."

"Shaun hardly fits that bill, and neither does his car!" said Jan dryly. "You know, Becky, however much you love someone, it is possible to grow out of a relationship. Some things, well, even if they're good, they're just not meant to last for ever..."

"Philosophy at this time of the morning! Help!" groaned Fi, shuffling into the kitchen with her eyes half-closed. "Ooh, I've got a terrible headache! Is there any coffee in the pot?"

"Plenty. It's just made," said Becky, pushing the pot over towards her. Fi poured herself a mugful and took two aspirins out of her dressing-gown pocket.

"Good party, eh, girls?" she said, gulping her coffee.

"Yes," said Becky. "It was a good party."

Except that it's left me even more mixed-up than I was before, she said to herself silently. Is Jan right? Am I growing out of my relationship with Nick? Growing away from him, while he's stuck at home and I'm in London? Or am I just growing up? Jan was watching her anxiously. Becky smiled at her.

"It's OK," she said softly.

Jan smiled back. She had always been outspoken, it was one of the things Becky liked most about her. Jan would always say what she thought. If you wanted an honest opinion, she'd give you one. Even if, sometimes, the truth hurt...

But was it the truth, this time?

The girls spent a lazy Sunday reading the papers and going for a stroll by the river in the afternoon. When Jan left to catch her train, loaded up with all her Christmas shopping, Becky gave her a hug.

"See you at Christmas!" she said, her voice muffled in Jan's scarf.

"Yes, see you, Becky! And thanks! I've had a fantastic weekend."

Jan hadn't mentioned Shaun or Nick, or even Paul, again, and Becky certainly wasn't going to say anything. What was there to say, anyway?

Shaun rang her in the office on Monday to thank her for the party and to ask her if she wanted to see another of the bands his company managed, who were gigging later in the week.

"They're not a bit like Rags. More sort of dancey," he told her. "They're fun, though. Want to come along?"

Becky said she did, and then proceeded to bury herself in work. It wasn't difficult. Linda was away with a nasty dose of flu, and Sandie Johnson was sniffling too, which made her even more sarcastic and snappy than usual.

"I've got to be better by Friday," she moaned. "I'm flying to Paris for the weekend to interview Chantal Courier!"

Becky made a mental note to keep out of Sandie's way until she was better. The last thing I need is her going on at me, she thought. Luckily, she had plenty to do. Her interview with Jacqui the pop singer had to be written up, and one of the ballet companies had put her in touch with a young dancer. Jade was away, on a catalogue shoot in the Gambia, but she was due back on Wednesday.

Her date with Shaun was for Friday night. She went into the office on Friday to find Linda still away, Paula in a panic because there was a deadline looming, and Sandie, still sniffling, about to set off for Paris.

"I'd rather be at home with a mug of hot lemon and a good book," she groaned. For once, Becky felt really sorry for her, red-nosed and coughing. She looked so miserable.

"Good luck. I hope the interview goes well," she said politely.

"Thanks," said Sandie coldly, unwrapping another cough sweet.

Not long after she had left, Paula went into a meeting with the Editor, leaving Becky alone in the office. She finished the filing she was doing and sat back, debating whether to make herself a cup of tea. Then she frowned. What was that leather-covered wallet on Sandie's desk? Surely it wasn't…"

She jumped up and went to look. It was Sandie's passport! Whatever shall I do? she thought. Whatever will Sandie do? She can't get to Paris without a passport!

She glanced at her watch. Sandie had been gone about half an hour. If she got a cab, with the passport, she could catch up with Sandie at Heathrow – just! She grabbed her coat, her bag, and the passport, and rushed out of the office.

"Fi," she gasped as she passed her friend's desk. "Sandie's forgotten her passport! I'll have to take it to the airport, fast!"

Fi never panicked. She often said that someone in the office had to stay calm and there were always plenty of crises on a magazine!

"Don't worry," she said. "I'll order you a cab from the company we have our account with. I've got Sandie's flight number here somewhere…"

It seemed like the slowest journey Becky had ever been on. There were red traffic lights, road-works, hold-ups, traffic jams, and big, slow lorries crawling along, while she sat in the back of the cab chewing her fingernails and watching the minutes tick by. She almost fell out of the cab at the airport and rushed into the terminal, looking for Sandie. Suppose I can't find her, she thought frantically. Suppose … oh, no! Suppose she's realized she forgot her passport and gone back for it? She'll miss her flight, her interview…

"Becky?"

She hardly recognized the pale girl with the tear-stained face as the cool, collected, sophisticated Sandie who always seemed to be sneering at her.

"Thank goodness I've found you!" she cried with a sigh of relief. "I've just had an awful thought, that you might have gone back for it!" She handed the passport over. Miracle of miracles, Sandie actually smiled, and gave her a hug.

"Thanks, Becky," she said sincerely. "I rang Fi as soon as I realized I'd left it behind and she told me you'd spotted it and were on your way. I can't tell you how grateful I am. That was quick thinking!"

146

Becky felt embarrassed. "Oh ... well, you'd have done the same for me," she mumbled.

"I'm not sure that I would," said Sandie sheepishly. "I haven't treated you very well, have I? In fact, I've been a real bitch!"

"Um," said Becky, not knowing what to say.

"I wanted my sister to have your job, you see," Sandie went on. "So I kidded myself you were no good and that Alison would have done better. But ... I was wrong. You're one of the team now, Becky!"

"Thanks, Sandie!" Becky said.

"It's a real weight off my mind, you know," she confided to Shaun, later that evening. "It's been horrible working with someone I just knew was watching for me to make the tiniest mistake!"

"Well, she'll be all right now," Shaun said. "It just goes to show, anyone can make a mistake, even a stupid one like forgetting their passport."

"I know. But she made me feel it was my fault, that I really wasn't cut out to be a journalist at all," said Becky. "My three months' trial with the magazine is up next week. I've got to go and see the Editor!"

Shaun patted her hand. "I've told you, Becky. You're doing brilliantly!" he said. "The sky's the limit for a girl like you. You've come so far, so fast, when you think that this time last year you were still at school!"

Becky's smile faded. This time last year, she thought. She and Jan and Nick and Pete Ransome and a couple of the others had been organizing the

Sixth Form Christmas Disco. She and Nick had only been together a couple of months. We were so happy then, she thought with a pang of nostalgia. We had so many plans, we were going to go to college in the same town, we were sure we were going to be together for ever...

For ever, she thought, her eyes filling with tears. For ever is a long, long time...

"Becky, what is it?" said Shaun, his face full of concern.

She heaved a deep sigh. "Oh, nothing. I was just thinking about this time last year!"

He looked at her quizzically. "Happy memories?"

She hesitated, then nodded. He was silent for a moment and then said, "Come on, I'll take you home."

He didn't say much on the drive back to Camberwell, but when the van drew up outside the flat and he switched the engine off, he turned to face her.

"Becky," he said seriously. "Becky, I..."

His face was centimetres from her own. Becky sat still, mesmerized. He's going to kiss me, she thought, and I'm not going to stop him. I want him to kiss me. I've wanted it for so long. Too long.

Then his warm lips were on hers and his arms were around her, holding her as though he never wanted to let her go. She felt his hair, crisp beneath her fingers, smelled the masculine scent of his skin. Then he broke away.

"I ... I'm sorry, Becky," he gasped. "I've tried, I really have. I shouldn't ... I know you've got this other bloke..."

He turned away from her, gripping the steering-wheel.

"I never wanted to say this, Becky! But you'll have to choose. I don't want you as a friend, I want you as a girlfriend! So ... it's him or me!"

10

"Becky? Say something!" Shaun pleaded.

Becky shook her head, tears stinging her eyes. She couldn't even look at Shaun. Part of her longed to tell him how much he meant to her. Part of her wanted to fling herself into his arms and forget everything in the warmth of his kisses...

But she couldn't do that. She was Nick's girlfriend. Wasn't she? It was all very well for Jan to say that what the eye didn't see, the heart didn't grieve over, but Becky just wasn't that kind of person. She loved and respected both Nick and Shaun too much to cheat on either one of them.

"I see," said Shaun coolly, after a long silence. "Well, I guess that's telling me, Becky. It's my own fault, anyway. You said you only thought of me as a friend. Stupid of me, to imagine I could change your mind!"

"Oh, Shaun, I'm sorry," Becky faltered.

He shrugged. "Ah, well, can't win 'em all, can I?" he said lightly. "Whoever he is, Becky, he's a lucky guy! Let me know if you do change your mind, won't you?"

A huge, choking sob rose in Becky's chest. I can't bear it, she thought. I can't bear Shaun being so ... so self-sacrificing, such a good loser. I'd rather he was angry with me, furious, jealous ... like Nick would be!

"Shaun, I..." she began. She looked up at him. His hurt expression and rueful half-smile tore at her heart. "Goodbye, Shaun!" she gasped.

She opened the car door and fled up the front path as though wolves were after her, tears pouring down her cheeks as she fumbled for her door-key.

"Becky? Whatever's happened? Are you all right?"

Ruth, Fi and Jade were all up watching the late-night movie. Ruth jumped up and put her arms round Becky, Fi brought her a mug of cocoa, and Jade listened, wide-eyed, as Becky sobbed out her story.

"Well, if you're sure you've done the right thing," Jade said doubtfully.

"But that's just it!" gulped Becky. "I don't know if I have! Shaun's so ... so ... I mean, I really like him! But I can't just dump Nick, not after all he's been through..."

Becky spent a miserable weekend, even though the girls dragged her out to a new club on Saturday night, and she was asked for her phone number by no less than three different guys! It's always the same, she thought forlornly. When you're looking for romance, it's nowhere in sight!

When you're not, when it's absolutely the last thing you need, guys come running! Every time she thought of Shaun, it was all she could do not to burst into tears again. She even phoned Nick, but according to his mum he was out playing football, and he didn't call her back.

I'm giving up boys altogether, she thought wretchedly. From now on, I'm going to concentrate on my career!

That, at least, seemed to be going well. On Monday, she had her meeting with the Editor. To her surprise, the Managing Director, Harvey Preston, was in Sue's office when she tapped, rather nervously, on the door.

"Oh, Becky! Come on in!" said Sue. Becky had always been rather in awe of her, with her smart designer suits and well-cut blonde bob. Since her very first interview, she hadn't seen much of her, though Sue always smiled and said "Hi, Becky! Everything all right?" when their paths did cross.

"Don't look so worried," said Harvey Preston kindly.

Becky relaxed and managed to smile. I shouldn't worry, she thought. Linda's told me several times that she's pleased with me.

"Becky, I wanted to let you know that we're all very happy with your work," said the Editor.

"Thank you very much!" Becky replied, blushing.

"Linda tells me you're doing more writing these days. That pop interview you did came out really well," Sue went on. "But it's not just that, Becky. Producing a magazine is all about teamwork.

Everyone has to pull their weight and not mind doing the boring things like filing and going through the post, cheerfully and without grumbling. We don't need prima-donna types here!"

For a fleeting moment, Becky thought of Sandie Johnson.

"So," said Harvey, "we both wanted to let you know that you've come through your three months' trial with flying colours! From now on, Becky, you're a permanent member of the team. Congratulations!"

He shook Becky's hand, and so did Sue.

"Thank you!" Becky said, feeling a huge grin stretching right across her face. "I ... I really love the job, you know. I dreamed of working on a magazine, when I was at school, and it's every bit as much fun as I thought it would be!"

Sue and Harvey both laughed. "I hope you'll always feel that way about it," Sue said.

Becky went back to the Features Department in a happy daze. Even the thought of Shaun and Nick couldn't dim the glow she felt. At least *something* in my life is going right, she thought.

"Good news?" said Paula, looking up from her computer screen.

"Yes! Well..." said Becky, suddenly feeling embarrassed, "it looks like I shall be staying on. My three months' trial is up!"

To her astonishment, Paula, Sandie and Linda all started clapping!

"I'll ... I'll make us all a cup of tea," Becky stammered, to cover her confusion.

"Good idea," said Sandie warmly. "And I'll pop

out to the bakery and treat us all to doughnuts. This calls for a celebration!"

Becky saw Linda's eyebrows go up. She could hardly believe it herself. Sandie Johnson? Celebrating on Becky's behalf? Buying doughnuts? Whatever next? Still, she thought, it means everything's all right now. At work, anyway...

But that didn't help as Christmas approached, the magazine office became busier and crazier, and party invitations started to come in. Becky was invited to several record-company parties, but decided not to go in case she ran into Shaun. I couldn't bear to see him with anyone else, she thought. I couldn't bear to see him, full stop.

She made plans to go home the day before Christmas Eve. Harvey Preston was treating the magazine staff to lunch at a posh West End restaurant that day, so she booked a seat on an early evening train.

"Of course Dad will meet you, love," her mum told her on the phone. "And Emily's almost beside herself with excitement!"

Becky heard the clatter as her little sister grabbed the phone.

"Hello, Becky! Do you know what? Farver Christmas is coming next week!"

"Only to good girls, Emily!" Becky reminded her.

"I am a good girl! Vewy, vewy good!" Emily said indignantly.

Somehow, Becky's heart wasn't in the Christmas preparations. She went out with Ruth, Jade and Fi, helped the girls decorate the flat, wrapped her presents, listened to Christmas carols on the radio – and wished that none of it was happening, or that she was still Emily's age and young enough to get excited about Santa and Rudolph, Dancer and Prancer, Donner and Blitzen.

I'm too old for fairy-tales, she thought sadly. I don't believe in happy endings any more.

Jan phoned, full of plans for the fun they would have over the holiday. She didn't mention Shaun, and neither did Becky. I'll tell her when I get home, Becky thought. Nick phoned to ask her what she wanted for Christmas. Becky was in a quandary. She knew Nick didn't have much money, and anyway, she had always believed presents should be surprises.

"Oh, I don't know, Nick," she said. "Surprise me!"

"I'm hopeless at that sort of thing, you know I am!" Nick grumbled.

"Well, use your imagination!" said Becky. "I'll be home on Wednesday night, so how about meeting on Thursday?"

Nick hesitated. "Well, all right," he said in the end, "but I did say I'd go out with Darren..." Becky's heart sank.

"But maybe he could bring Tara along, make up a foursome," Nick went on.

"Tara? Who's Tara? I thought his girlfriend was called Mitzi?" said Becky.

"No, he dumped her. This one's called Tara ... or it might be Lara..."

"Or even Sara ... or possibly Kara..." giggled Becky. There was a pained silence at the other end of the line.

"Are you taking the mickey?" Nick demanded.

"No, of course not, you idiot! I was joking!"

"Oh."

But Nick still sounded huffy, and soon rang off. What's the matter with him? Becky thought. I was only joking!

Even a riotous Christmas lunch with the rest of the *Ace* staff didn't help. Whatever happened to the Christmas spirit? Becky thought, as she sat on the train home. It seems to have passed me by this year!

She felt better once she had got home. The house smelled of freshly-baked mince pies. Emily had insisted on having home-made paper-chains everywhere. They kept falling down and her dad had to pin them back up, time after time! Cards festooned the mantelpiece and hung on strings round the walls. It's good to be home, Becky thought, in spite of everything.

Shaun had sent her a card. Her heart thumped as she opened it. He'd sent it from the office and it was just signed "Shaun". What did it mean? Was she forgiven? Did he still feel the same about her? Could they even be friends again, one day? Becky shoved the card back into its envelope and put it at the bottom of her suitcase. She didn't want to be reminded of Shaun. I did the right thing, she told herself.

Nick greeted her with a big hug and a kiss when he came round on Christmas Eve. He said hello to her parents and whisked her out to Darren's car. Becky went cold. It was like a re-run of that earlier evening that had ended so disastrously.

Tara, or Lara, was another fluffy blonde in a low-cut dress, looking so much like Mitzi that they could have been sisters. Darren still drove too fast, and they ended up at a club in the middle of town where Becky had never been.

"Darren's brother's the manager here, so we get in free!" murmured Nick as they went past two tough-looking bouncers on the door. The music pounded out and Becky sighed to herself. Were she and Nick ever going to get the chance for a heart-to-heart?

"Good club, huh?" Darren said, as he ordered a round of drinks.

Becky smiled and nodded.

"It might not be what you London types are used to, but it's the best this town has to offer!" said Nick bitterly.

Becky laughed. "I don't have the money to go to top West End clubs very often," she said. "The girls in the flat and I normally just go out locally..."

There was an awkward pause.

"Nick says you work on *Ace* magazine," gushed Tara. "That must be ever so exciting!"

"Well, sometimes," said Becky cautiously.

"Have you ever met anyone famous?"

"Not really. I've only just started doing pop interviews. But I did interview a guy from a band called Rags," Becky told her.

"Rags? Aren't they in the charts?"

"Yes. Top Twenty this week," said Becky proudly. She had been watching the progress of Rags' single with her fingers crossed, feeling as though she was personally involved!

"Their singer's cute, isn't he?" Tara giggled.

"Paul? Oh, he's really nice. He was the one I interviewed, actually," said Becky.

"You didn't!" Tara breathed. "Aren't you lucky? I wish interviewing hunky guys was part of *my* job!"

Becky was about to reply that it was only a very tiny part of hers when she saw Nick's face. His lower lip was thrust out, his eyes were hooded, and he looked furious.

"What is it?" she asked him, when Darren and Tara had gone off to dance.

"Can't you ever shut up about that job?" Nick hissed angrily. "I'm tired of hearing about models and pop stars and all the rest of it. You're turning into a real poser, a name-dropper..."

"No, I'm not!" Becky snapped back. "I only mentioned it because Tara asked me. And Paul's not really a pop star, he's only just had his first record in the charts..."

"Well, I don't want to hear about him!" Nick snarled.

Becky opened her mouth to argue, but then sat back, defeated. A night club wasn't the place, and Christmas Eve wasn't the time, but she knew she and Nick were going to have to sort this out. It's my job, Becky thought. I'm a journalist, that's what I do, whether Nick likes it or not. I'm probably going to be doing more pop interviews, and if people like Tara ask me about them, what am I supposed to say? Nick knows I always wanted to be a journalist. Why isn't he pleased for me, proud of me?

Shaun was, said a small, disloyal voice in her head. Shaun used to say that the sky was the limit for someone like me. So why does Nick try to drag me down all the time?

Suddenly, Nick reached across the table and squeezed her hand. "Dance with me, Becky?" he said.

Becky hesitated for a moment, then stood up. What else can I do? she thought. We're in a club, it's Christmas Eve, goodwill to all men, and all that...

She and Nick left early, Becky remembering that she would be woken at six, or earlier, by Emily! They strolled along the night-time streets, Nick's arm resting gently around Becky's shoulders, their disagreement forgotten. They passed the cinema where they'd been on their first date, the Pizza House where Nick had taken her to celebrate their six-month "anniversary", the town-centre stop where they'd caught the bus to school so often. So many memories, Becky thought.

"What are you doing tomorrow?" Nick asked her.

Becky giggled. "What d'you think? Up at the crack of dawn with Emily, presents round the tree, roast turkey, the Queen's speech..."

"I mean, shall I come round in the afternoon? My mum and dad generally doze off after the Queen, so they won't miss me. I could give you your present and we could go for a walk or something."

"Good idea," said Becky. "We can walk off some of the Christmas pud and mince pies!"

They strolled on companionably, not saying much. I wish it could always be like this, Becky thought. Peaceful. Easy. Not worrying about what to say next, or if Nick will think I'm a poser...

When they arrived at her front door, the house was in darkness. Nick swung her round to face him.

"Merry Christmas, darling," he said huskily.

Darling, Becky thought. He's never called me darling before! She reached up and kissed him on the cheek.

"I've got to go," she whispered. "I need a bit of sleep before Emily comes in and jumps on me with her stocking!"

Nick looked as though he was going to say something else, but in the end he just gave her a hug and murmured, "Night! I'll see you tomorrow!"

It seemed to Becky as though she had only just closed her eyes when her bedside light was snapped on and a small figure appeared, carrying a brightly-coloured Christmas stocking crammed with parcels.

"Becky! BECKY! Farver Christmas has been! An' ... an' ... he's eaten his mince pie all up, an' so has Rudolph eaten the carrot I left for him!" Emily cried.

"Sorry, Becky," said Mrs Rivers, yawning, as she handed Becky a cup of tea. "I told Emily she wasn't to wake you..."

"What's the time?" murmured Becky groggily, surfacing.

"Twenty to seven. We haven't done too badly. I

can remember you waking your dad and me up at ten past five, when you were about Emily's age!"

Becky helped Emily open her parcels, wished her parents a Merry Christmas, and the day began. It was crisp and cold and sunny, perfect winter weather, and Becky found she was looking forward to seeing Nick in the afternoon. We'll be able to talk, at last, she thought.

He arrived just as the Queen's Speech was finishing, and handed her a tiny parcel. "This is for you," he said. "Happy Christmas, Mr Rivers, Mrs Rivers ... Emily!"

"Farver Christmas came, Nick," Emily told him. "He brought me a dollies' pram, an' a Polly Pocket, an' a story-book..."

"Did he?" said Nick absent-mindedly, his eye on Becky as she unwrapped her present and took out a tiny, delicate gold chain with a flower pendant on the end.

"Nick, it's beautiful! Thank you very, very much!" she said.

"Here, let me put it on." He fastened the clasp round the back of her neck and stood for a moment, smiling down at her. He does care, Becky thought.

"Let's go for that walk," he said.

The park was almost deserted, except for a few excited children trying out new bikes and roller-blades. Becky and Nick walked towards the bandstand, their breath curling away from them like smoke in the icy air.

"Becky," said Nick, "I want to ask you something!"

She turned to him enquiringly. He looked ... what? Shy? Embarrassed? What *is* this? she thought, bewildered.

"Becky, would you ... that is ... had you thought about ... would you like us to get engaged?" Nick said.

Becky was so astonished that she could only stare at him, open-mouthed. After a silence that seemed to last hours, she managed to croak, *"Engaged?"*

"Yes." Nick laughed uneasily. "Don't look so horrified!"

"I ... I ... I'm not ... I'm just, well, surprised..." Becky gasped.

"But why? I mean ... we've been together more than a year now ... it's sort of the next natural step, isn't it? I ... I don't really like you being down there in London without me, Becky! All those other guys ... if you had a ring on, well, they'd know you belonged to me, wouldn't they? I mean, that we belonged together..."

Becky looked at him, her thoughts in a whirl. Engaged? She had truly never thought about it. An engagement meant marriage, settling down, buying a flat, starting a family. All things that she wanted to do, looked forward to doing – one day, in the far distant future, when she'd had fun, and travelled, and become an established and successful journalist. But not now, not yet...

And not with Nick!

She shook her head, the slow realization creeping into her heart like a splinter of ice. She didn't want to marry Nick!

"Nick, I..." she began feebly.

Eagerly, he interrupted her. "Oh, I know what you're thinking. You're worried about your job and everything, aren't you? But I wouldn't want to get married yet anyway. When I've got the job in my uncle's garage, and we've saved up a bit, enough for a deposit on our own place..."

"It sounds like you've got it all worked out," said Becky faintly.

He laughed. "Well, you don't want to work on that magazine for ever, do you?" he said. "And why scrimp and scrape for a grotty flat in London when you can buy a really nice house out here for the same money? Darren says..."

Becky looked at him, in his familiar jeans and old suede jacket, his sherry-brown eyes and untidy hair, and it was like looking at a stranger. He just doesn't understand, she thought. I don't know him any more. He's changed, he's not the same. Or maybe it's me...

Suddenly, she remembered what Jan had said.

"Some things aren't meant to last for ever ... they may be good, right for the moment, but not for always. You can grow out of loving someone..."

Oh, Jan, you were right, she thought, her eyes blurring with tears. Nick and I, we're just not the same people any more! I've just been clinging on to old dreams, old memories, old loyalties...

Nick was looking at her expectantly. "Well," he said, "what do you think?"

Becky took a deep breath. She knew what she had to say. It was the hardest thing she had ever done – and yet, in another way, it was easy, because it was right. "I'm so sorry, Nick," she said in a shaken voice. "I don't want to get engaged!"

Nick drew back slightly, frowning. "But why? Why, Becky?"

He swallowed hard. "Are you … are you saying you don't love me any more?"

"I … I…" said Becky miserably, brushing away the tears with the back of her hand. *Was* she saying that? Choosing her words carefully, she said, "Nick, you know I'll always love you. In a way. But, please try and understand. We … we don't seem to want the same things any more. Getting engaged, settling down … it's not for me, Nick! Not yet. I love my job, and I like living in London, and I want to go on in my career, right to the top, or as near to it as I can get…"

Nick made a harsh sound of disgust and turned away from her. "I knew it," he muttered through clenched teeth. "The glamour, the bright lights, mixing with posh people and rock stars, it's really got to you, hasn't it, Becky? A small-town guy like me, well, I'm just not good enough!"

Becky closed her eyes. How could she ever make him understand? It was nothing to do with glamour or bright lights, nothing to do with Nick not being "good enough". It was just that she was growing up, moving on, breaking away. There was a whole new world out there, and she, Becky, wanted to be part of it.

"It's not that at all…" she began wretchedly.

He took hold of her wrist in a grip that hurt. "Then what is it? Tell me! Is there someone else? Another guy? If there is, I'll … I'll…"

164

Becky shook her head. "No," she said truthfully. "No, there's no one."

There was a long silence. Across the park, children squealed in excitement as they tried out their new toys. This is the worst Christmas of my life, Becky thought.

"You really mean it, don't you?" Nick said.

Becky nodded dumbly.

"I hope you won't regret it!" he warned.

I'm regretting it right now, this minute, Becky thought. But, all the same, I know I'm right. Memories, gratitude, pity, a sort of love, I feel all those things for Nick, but it's not enough. Not any more...

She shook her head.

"That's it, then," he said savagely. "Goodbye, Becky!"

"Goodbye, Nick," she breathed. "And ... good luck!" She fumbled in her coat pocket for a tissue. When she looked up again, Nick had gone. Somehow, she managed to get herself home.

"Is that you, Becky?" her mother called from the kitchen. "Take Nick through into the front room, love. There's mince pies and Christmas cake. I'm just waiting for the kettle to boil ... Becky?"

"Oh, Mum," Becky sobbed, "it's Nick ... it's all over!"

Mrs Rivers didn't ask any questions. She didn't say anything. Instead, she enfolded Becky in the warmest of hugs, as if she was no older than Emily. At least someone loves me, Becky thought miserably, even if I've made a total and complete mess of my love-life! Perhaps I shall end up as a crabby old spinster, with nothing in her life except her job...

"Rubbish! How *can* you say that!" exploded Jan, when Becky confided her fears the next day. "Honestly, Becky, I told you it was time you and Nick called it a day, didn't I? He's just not right for you any more!"

"Jan, you don't think I've turned into a poser, do you?" Becky asked anxiously.

Jan snorted. "No, of course you haven't. Nick's just jealous. Forget him, Becky! Now everything's OK for you and Shaun..."

Becky remembered she hadn't told Jan about Shaun. Slowly, she shook her head. "He's gone, too," she said. "Oh, Jan, I've lost them both! It's all such a mess!"

Jan's eyes widened. "You'd better tell me all about it," she said.

Becky told her. Jan listened sympathetically and then said, "I know what I'd do if I were you!"

"What?"

"Ring him up. Now. At home. Tell him you've changed your mind!"

Becky gasped. "Jan! I can't do that!"

"Why ever not?"

"Because ... because he's at his parents' and I don't have their number!"

"That's what Directory Enquiries is for. Where do they live?" said Jan, grabbing the phone.

"Um ... somewhere in Berkshire. Near Reading. Something Green ... Kipps Green, I think he said. But, Jan..."

"And what's his name? Carswell? There won't be

166

thousands of Carswells. Thank goodness he's not called Shaun Smith!" said Jan briskly, dialling.

"But, Jan..."

"Sssh!" said Jan, scribbling down the number the electronic voice gave her. "There you are!"

Becky took the scrap of paper between her fingers and thumb, as though it might burn her. "Jan, I *can't*! What can I say? He'll think I'm crazy!"

"No, he won't. He'll think you've changed your mind, that's all. Didn't he say he wanted you to choose between him and Nick?"

"Well ... yes, but..."

"So. You've chosen him! All you have to do is tell him! Come on, Becky, don't be a wimp!"

"I ... I could just wish him a happy Christmas, and thank him for his card, I suppose," Becky murmured.

"Becky!" said Jan threateningly. "Just dial the number! Go on, do it!"

Becky felt as though someone else's fingers were pressing the buttons, someone else's clammy hand was clinging to the phone, someone else's heart was thumping in her ears.

"Hello?" came a woman's voice.

"C-could I speak to Shaun, please? It's Becky!"

About two centuries seemed to drag by. Then, at last, she heard Shaun's incredulous voice.

"Becky? But how did you ... Becky?"

At the sound of his voice, all Becky's fears fell away. She felt as though she was bathed in sunlight. It's going to be all right, she thought. The future stretched ahead of her, bright with promise, Shaun at her side.

"Becky?" he said again.

It wasn't hard at all. It was easy. So very, very easy.

"I love you, Shaun," she said. "And ... Merry Christmas!"

"I love you, too," said Shaun.

Point Horror

Are you hooked on horror? Thrilled by fear? Then these are the books for you. A powerful series of horror fiction designed to keep you quaking in your shoes.

The Claw
Carmen Adams

The Bride
The Cemetery
D.E. Athkins

The Dead Game
Mother's Helper
A. Bates

The Surfer
Linda Cargill

The Cheerleader
The Return of the Vampire
The Vampire's Promise
Freeze Tag
Night School
The Perfume
The Stranger
Twins
Caroline B. Cooney

April Fools
Help Wanted
Fatal Secrets
The Lifeguard
The Mall
Teacher's Pet
Trick or Treat
Richie Tankersley Cusick

Camp Fear
My Secret Admirer
Silent Witness
The Body
The Stalker
The Window
Carol Ellis

Vampire's Love
1. Blood Curse
2. Blood Spell
Janice Harrell

Funhouse
Prom Date
The Accident
The Invitation
The Fever
The Train
Diane Hoh

Sweet Sixteen
Francesca Jeffries

Driver's Dead
The Yearbook
Peter Lerangis

The Watcher
Lael Littke

Hide and Seek
Jane McFann

Point Horror

The Forbidden Game:
1. The Hunter
2. The Chase
3. The Kill
L.J. Smith

Amnesia
Dream Date
Second Sight
The Boy Next Door
The Diary
The Waitress
Sinclair Smith

Spring Break
The Mummy
The Phantom
Barbara Steiner

Beach House
Beach Party
Call Waiting
Halloween Night
Halloween Night II
Hit and Run
The Baby-sitter
The Baby-sitter II
The Baby-sitter III
The Baby-sitter IV
The Boyfriend
The Dead Girlfriend
The Girlfriend
The Hitchhiker
The Snowman
The Witness
R.L. Stine

Thirteen Tales of Horror
Thirteen More Tales of
Horror
Thirteen Again
Various

P●INT CRiME

If you like Point Horror, you'll love Point Crime!

Kiss of Death
School for Death
Peter Beere

Avenging Angel
Break Point
Deadly Inheritance
Final Cut
Shoot the Teacher
The Beat:
Missing Person
Black and Blue
Smokescreen
Asking For It
Dead White Male
Losers
David Belbin

Baa Baa Dead Sheep
Dead Rite
Jill Bennett

A Dramatic Death
Bored to Death
Margaret Bingley

Driven to Death
Patsy Kelly
Investigates:
A Family Affair
End of the Line
No Through Road
Accidental Death
Brotherly Love
Anne Cassidy

Overkill
Alane Ferguson

Deadly Music
Dead Ringer
Death Penalty
Dennis Hamley

Fade to Black
Stan Nicholls

Concrete Evidence
The Alibi
The Smoking Gun
Lawless and Tilley:
The Secrets of the Dead
Deep Waters
Malcolm Rose

Dance with Death
Jean Ure

13 Murder Mysteries
Various